The Art of Rasgueado

This is a comprehensive analysis of the rasgueado technique for classical and flamenco guitar including chapters on rhumba rhythms and the golpe technique

by Ioannis Anastassakis, MA.

1 2 3 4 5 6 7 8 9 0

© 2002 BY MEL BAY PUBLICATIONS, INC., PACIFIC, MO 63069.
ALL RIGHTS RESERVED. INTERNATIONAL COPYRIGHT SECURED. B.M.I. MADE AND PRINTED IN U.S.A.
No part of this publication may be reproduced in whole or in part, or stored in a retrieval system, or transmitted in any form or by any means, electronic, mechanical, photocopy, recording, or otherwise, without written permission of the publisher.

Visit us on the Web at www.melbay.com — E-mail us at email@melbay.com

Introduction by Juan Serrano

I met Ioannis Anastassakis in 1996, when he came to Fresno to pursue a Masters degree in Flamenco Guitar & History. From the moment that we met and I listened to him play, I knew he had something unique to offer to the flamenco guitar world.

This book is the proof of my thoughts. Ioannis studied and researched the rasgueado technique of every significant flamenco guitarist in the world. After extensive and elaborate research, he has compiled his work in an easy and understandable notation form, with excellent explanations of each rasgueado technique.

From this book, every flamenco & non-flamenco guitarist, from *aficionado* to professional, can learn everything about the rasgueado technique and its interpretation.

I sincerely congratulate Ioannis for his remarkable work and wish him good luck & success in his professional career.

Juan Serrano
Professor of Music
California State University, Fresno

Table of Contents

The Art of Rasgueado

The rasgueado technique is, without a doubt, the most impressive and characteristic element of the flamenco guitar. The first time I witnessed a flamenco guitarist perform, I was instantly mesmerized by the way he was moving his right hand and all the sounds he was producing simultaneously. It sounded to me as if 3 guitars were playing at the same time! The intricacies of his motions seemed endless; nevertheless, he was able to chain his rhythms in a seamless fashion that made complete musical sense.

In Spain, where flamenco originated, rasgueado means "strum". In English, the same word is used to express the characteristic kind of rhythmically complex strumming that is emblematic of the flamenco guitar.

The rasgueado techniques were originally developed out of necessity in order to accompany the flamenco dance and song. By strumming the guitar instead of plucking it, the guitarist could produce a much stronger, louder sound, and therefore could be heard above the resounding vocals of the singer and the throbbing footwork of the dancer. As the decades passed, the flaming flamenco virtuosos developed many different forms of rasgueados.

The reason for this extreme development was twofold: First, since most of the musical material played by the flamenco guitarist when accompanying dance and song was improvised, the player who had a specific idea about a particular rhythmic pattern was forced to invent his own way of executing it. Until now, there was no book or complete method to show how it was all done and explain the best fingerings to be used depending on the rhythmic subdivisions. So he made up his own!

The other reason, probably even more important, was that gypsy flamenco guitarists were always very secretive about their art. They would not teach their techniques or show their musical phrases to other guitar players under any circumstances, even refusing to perform when other guitar players were present! This made necessary the need for invention for the players that managed to hear these virtuosos play and were very inspired by them, but could not get a clear explanation on how these techniques were executed. They heard the rhythmic patterns as performed by the virtuosos and then went on trying to imitate them on their instruments, discovering their own patterns in order to produce what they hoped would be similar results. All this procedure resulted in a multitude of available rasgueado patterns that seems to baffle even the most knowledgeable flamenco guitar aficionados.

I pursued my graduate studies at California State University Fresno, concentrating on Flamenco Guitar, under the tutelage of Juan Serrano. Juan Serrano is one of the most notable concert flamenco guitarists, a musician extraordinarily adept on the performance stage, as well as a very accomplished and prolific educator. During my years of studying with him, a great amount of time was spent analyzing the different rasgueados he had developed himself and other ones he had learned from other players. After that, I studied with another celebrated flamenco educator, Juan Martin and followed seminars with Serranito, Paco Pena and Dennis Koster, one of the most notable students of Sabicas and Mario Escudero. I spend a significant amount of time analyzing and deciphering the techniques of the contemporary flamenco guitar prodigies, like Tomatito, Vincente Amigo, Rafael Riqueni and Gerardo Nunez, as well as tracking down people who had studied with the notable Diego del Gastor from Jerez de la Frontera, persuading them to share their unique knowledge with me. And it is this knowledge that I wish to share with all of you!

Throughout this book the following symbols will be used:

e - little finger

a - ring finger

m - middle finger

i - index finger

p - thumb

☐ - Golpe

˅ or ↓= Upstroke

˄ or ↑=Downstroke

On the Rumba technique patterns chapter:

N = Single note played with thumb

S = Slap technique

Preparatory Rasgueados

We will start with the simplest form of rasgueado, index downstroke. Here is the **index downstroke**, playing quarter notes over a static, first position E major chord.

Movement description: The thumb rests lightly on the top side of the 6th string. All other RH fingers are loosely curled in the palm in a very relaxed way, with the knuckles pointing downwards. Then the index finger is flicked downwards, strumming the guitar strings from bass to treble.

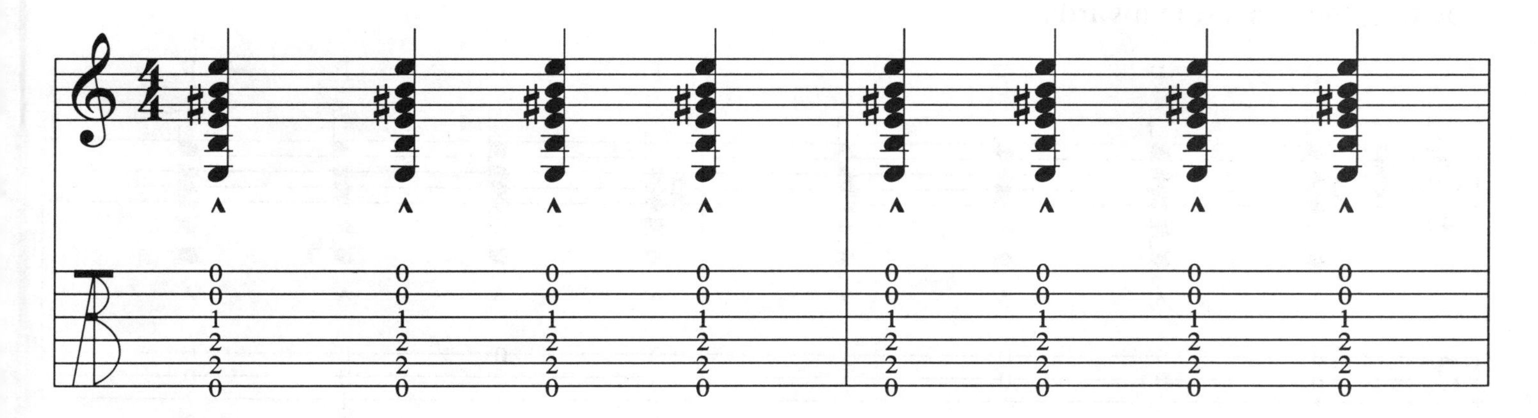

Then next step is the **index upstroke**, usually following the index downstroke. Now the index is playing 8th notes instead of quarter notes, with the downstroke on the downbeat and the upstroke on the upbeat. The same chord shape is used for ease of reference.

Movement description: The thumb rests lightly on the top side of the 6th string. All other RH fingers are loosely curled in the palm in a very relaxed way, with the knuckles pointing downwards. Then the index finger is flicked downwards, strumming the guitar strings from bass to treble, and then is drawn back, performing an upstroke on the upbeat.

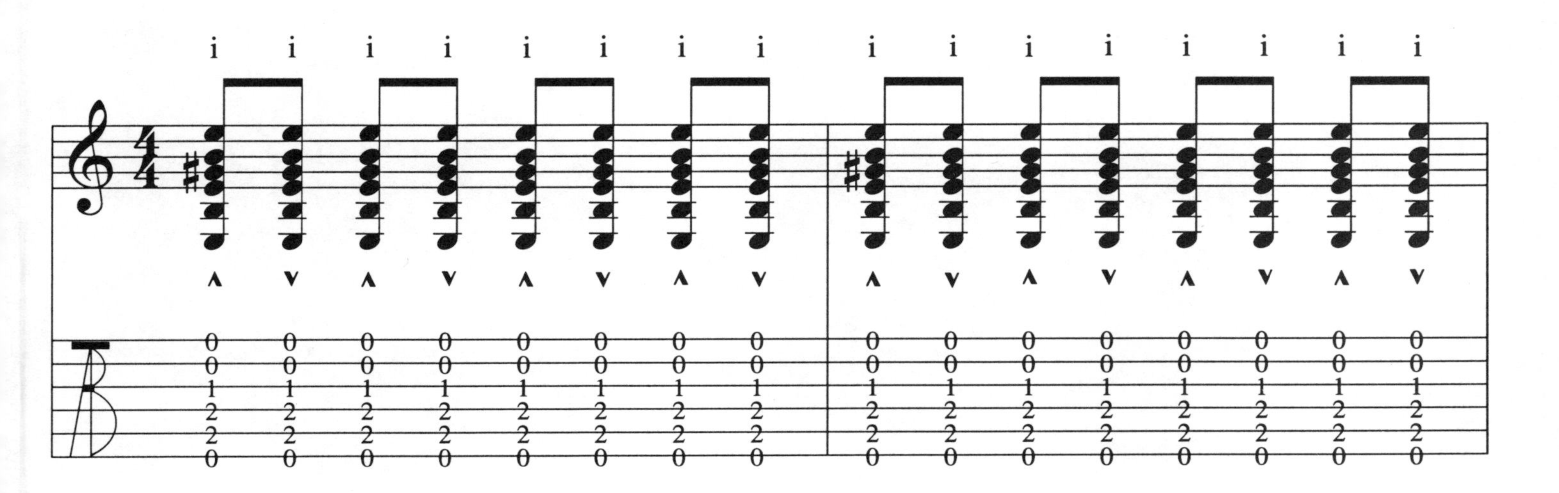

The same exact form will be repeated for the thumb. First the **thumb downstroke**; The main difference is that in this movement, the hand moves from the wrist, doing a downward motion, with the strings being attacked with a combination of nail and flesh. From now on we will be calling this position the "free" position, since the hand is not in contact with the strings prior to the beginning of the rasgueado and the thumb is not anchored to the 6ths string, or anywhere else.

Movement description: Here the hand position changes; the hand is free floating and there is no contact with the strings; it remains poised above them. The knuckles are pointing downwards, on a 45-degree angle to the strings. The thumb executes a downstroke, strumming the strings from bass to treble. The movement comes partially from the thumb joint and partially from rotating the wrist downwards.

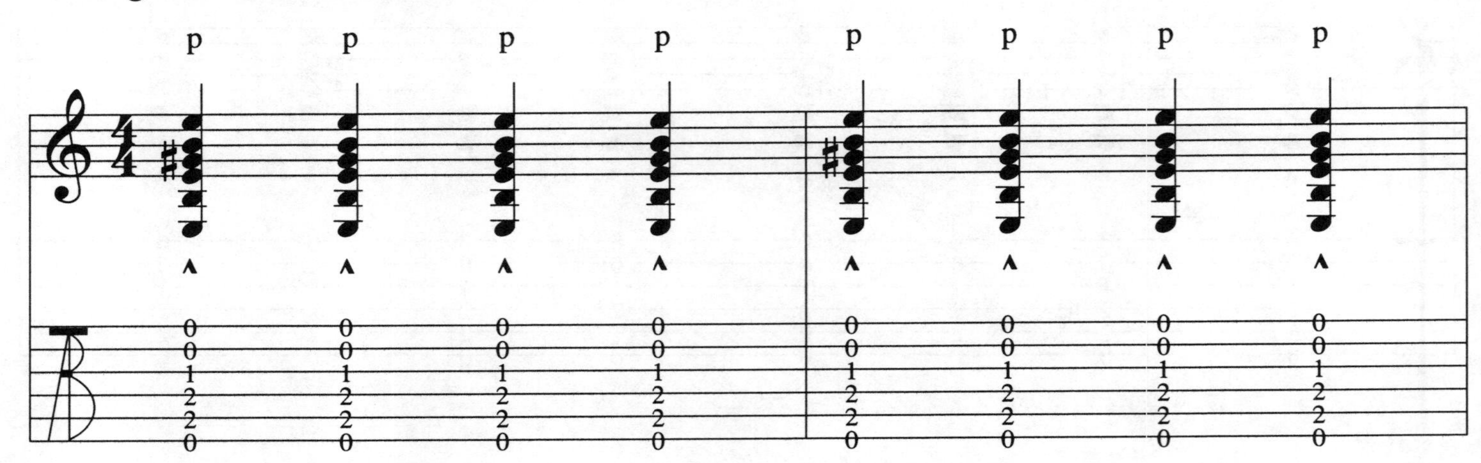

Then the **thumb upstroke**: In this movement, there is a definite preference on the high strings that get much more emphasized. The movement is a relaxed upward flick of the wrist, the strings being attacked with the upper side of the thumbnail.

Movement description: The hand is in the free position and there is no contact with the strings; it remains poised above them. The knuckles are pointing downwards, on a 45-degree angle to the strings. The thumb executes an upstroke, strumming the strings from treble to bass. The movement comes partially from the thumb joint and partially from rotating the wrist upwards.

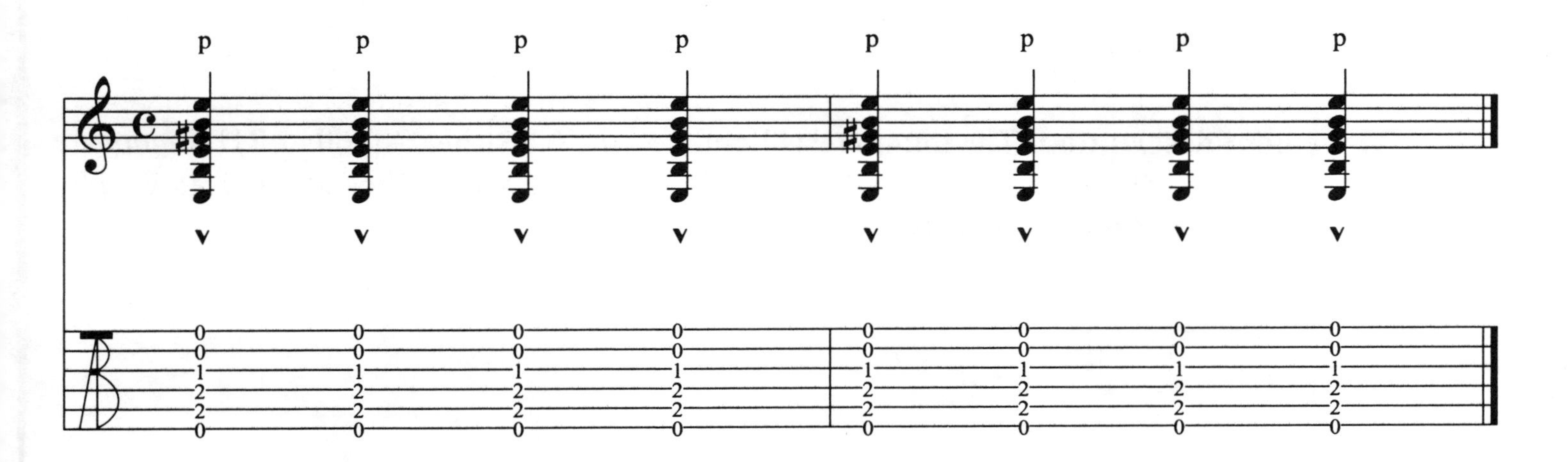

The final preparatory rasgueado is the **ma downstroke**. This is the same as the index downstroke, except it is performed with the middle and ring fingers loosely joined together;

Movement description: The thumb rests lightly on the 6th string. All other RH fingers are loosely curled in the palm in a very relaxed way. Then the middle and ring fingers are flicked downwards in a joined motion, strumming the guitar strings from bass to treble.

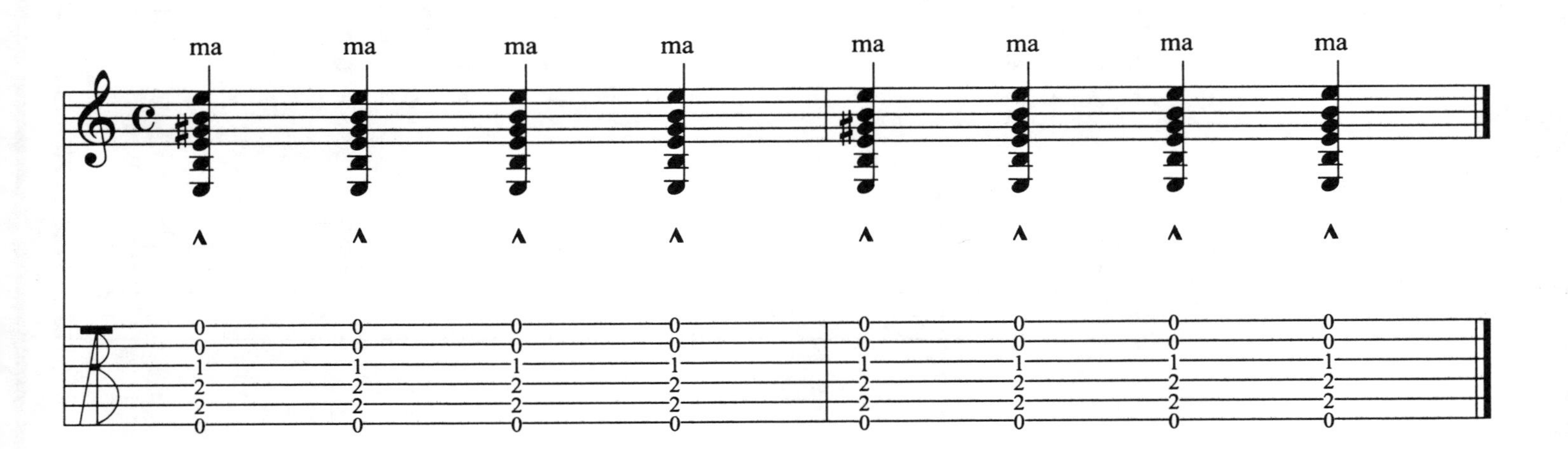

Ornamental rasgueados

The most widely used rasgueado form is, strangely enough, without a really specific rhythmic structure! It does not have a specific rhythm breakdown of 16th notes, triplets, quintuplets or sextuplets. It is used as an ornament with an accent on a specific beat, instead of a repeating rhythmic structure. For the sake of rhythmic clarity, it will be notated as triplets. However, I want to make it very clear that this rasgueado is an ORNAMENT, not a specific rhythmical form! Its execution slightly precedes the targeted beat and resolves exactly on the downbeat.

The **eami** rasgueado:

Movement description: The thumb rests lightly on the 6th string. All other RH fingers are loosely curled in the palm in a very relaxed way. Then the little finger is flicked out, followed by the ring, the middle and finally, exactly on the beat, the index finger.

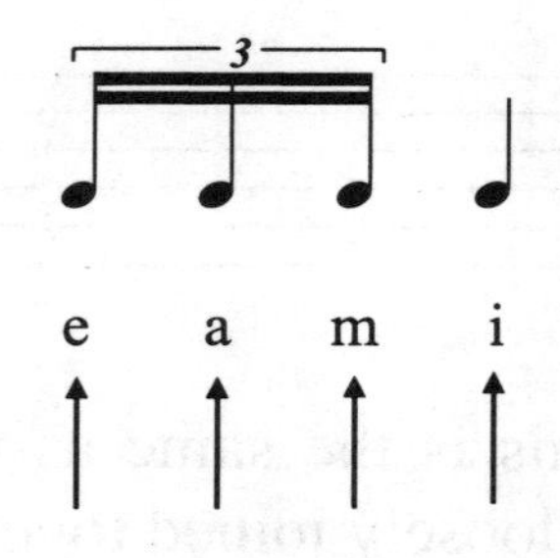

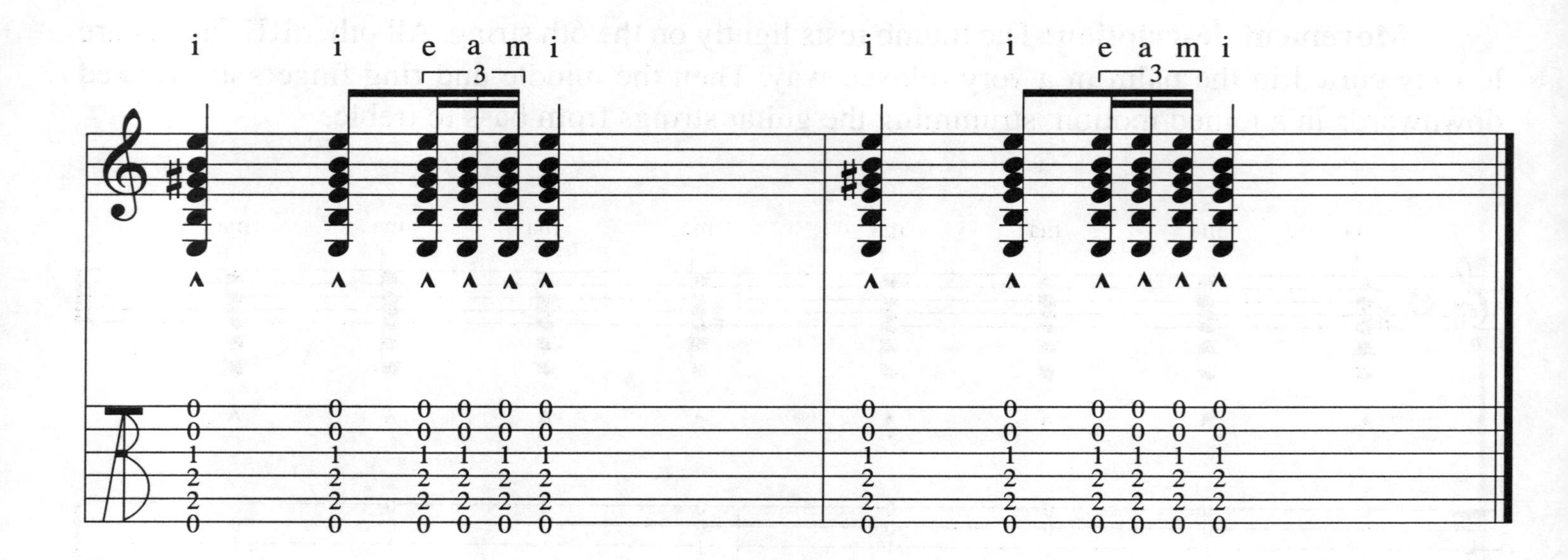

16th note traditional rasgueados

The **ieami** rasgueado:

This variation of the basic rasgueado was developed and honed to perfection by Juan Serrano. He developed it when he realized the need to have a consistent, rhythmically even rasgueado, that produces a steady stream of 16th or 32nd notes that will always correctly end on beat.

Movement description: The hand position is the same as the basic rasgueado with the thumb resting lightly on the 6th string. All other RH fingers are loosely curled in the palm in a very relaxed way. The index finger is flicked out, then the little finger, followed by the ring, the middle and finally, exactly on the beat, the index finger. VERY IMPORTANT: The secret to mastering this move is that at the same time the little finger strums, the index returns to its original position, poised and ready to strike again.

Here is an example with a duration of 2 beats:

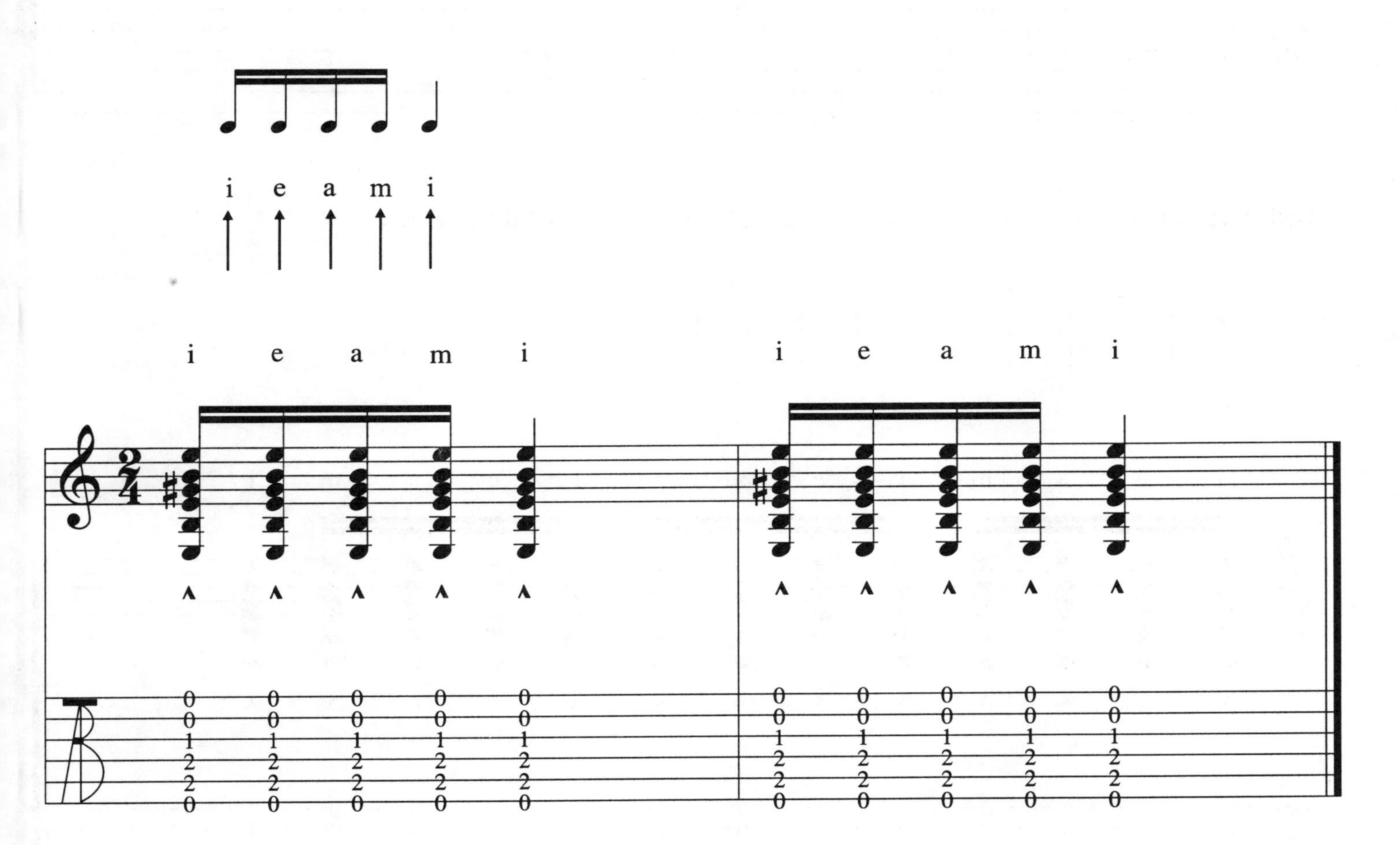

Here it is in the duration of 3 beats. Once again, each strum has the duration of a 16th note,

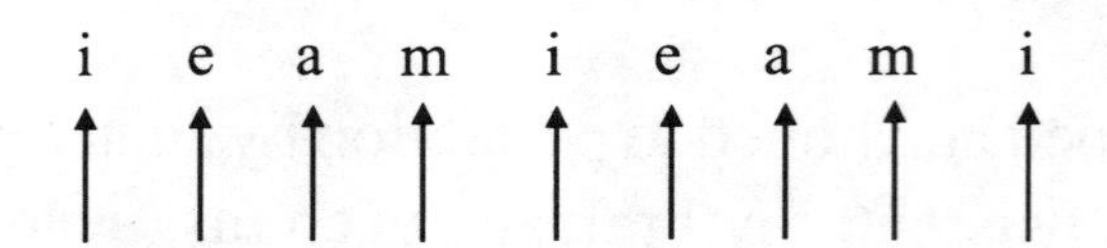

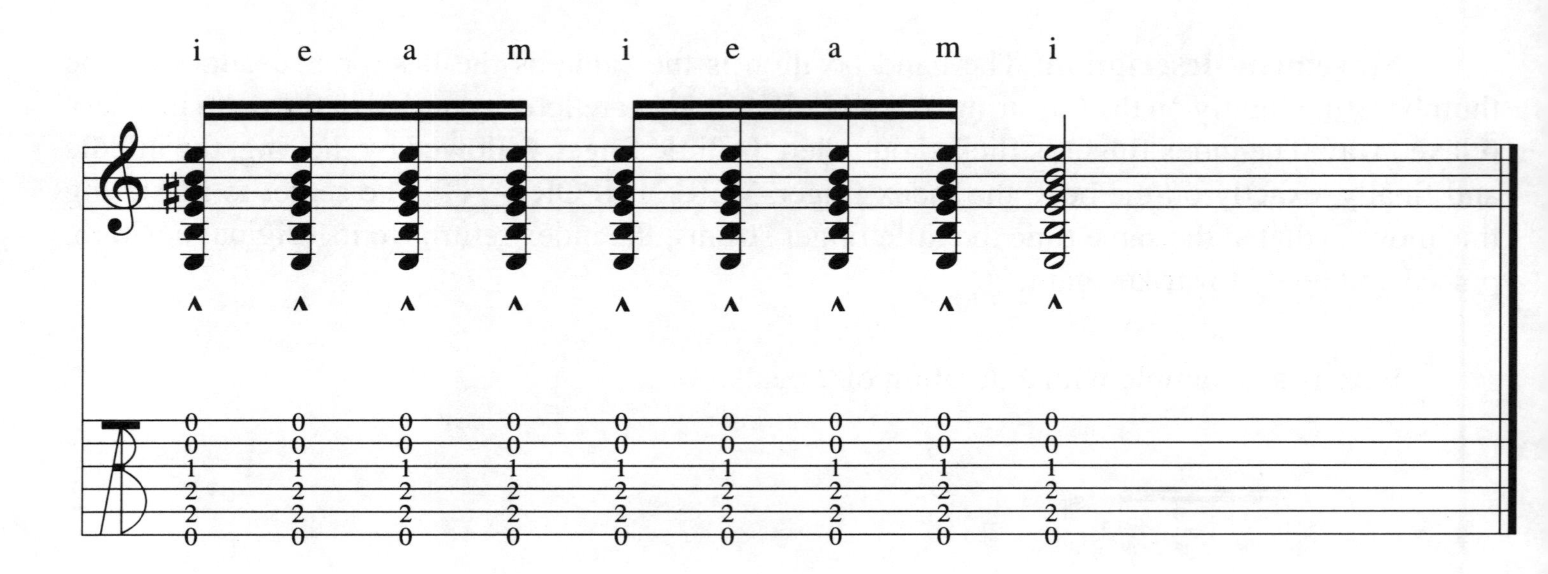

And here it is used in a continuous stream of 16th notes, totaling 4 beats.

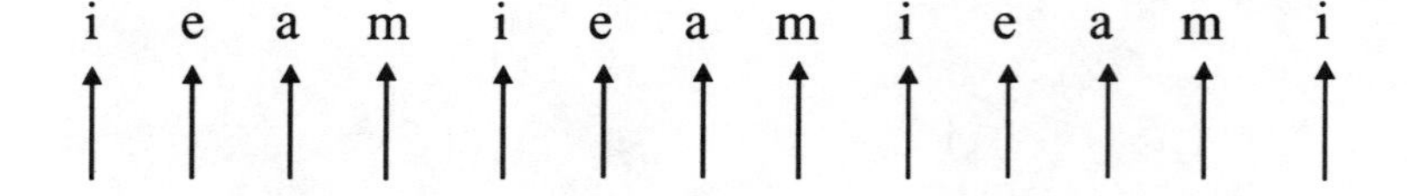

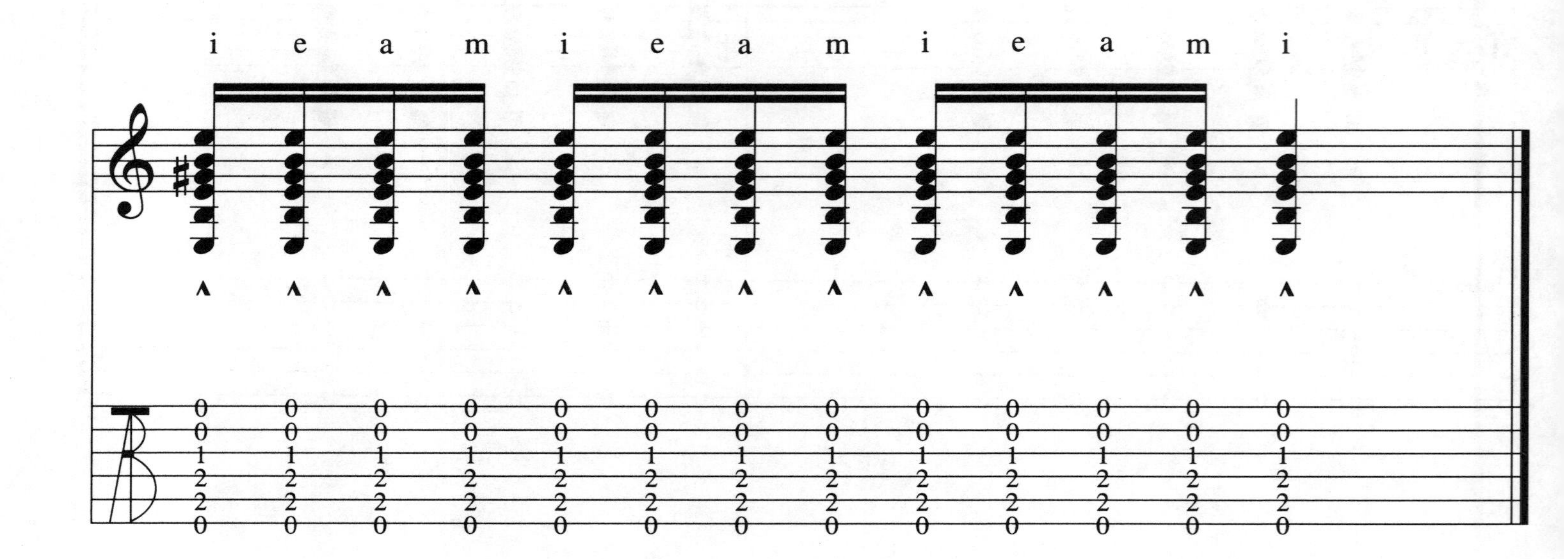

Therefore, we have a continuously recurring set of four 16th notes, during which the index always plays the 1st, the little finger always plays the 2nd, the ring finger always plays the 3rd and the middle finger always plays the 4th. This rasgueado is brilliant in its simplicity and can be executed evenly and clearly even by beginners with only a few months of guitar experience under their belt!

The same form can be used for 32nd notes (after considerable practice, though!). Here is an example of 32nd notes in 2 beats:

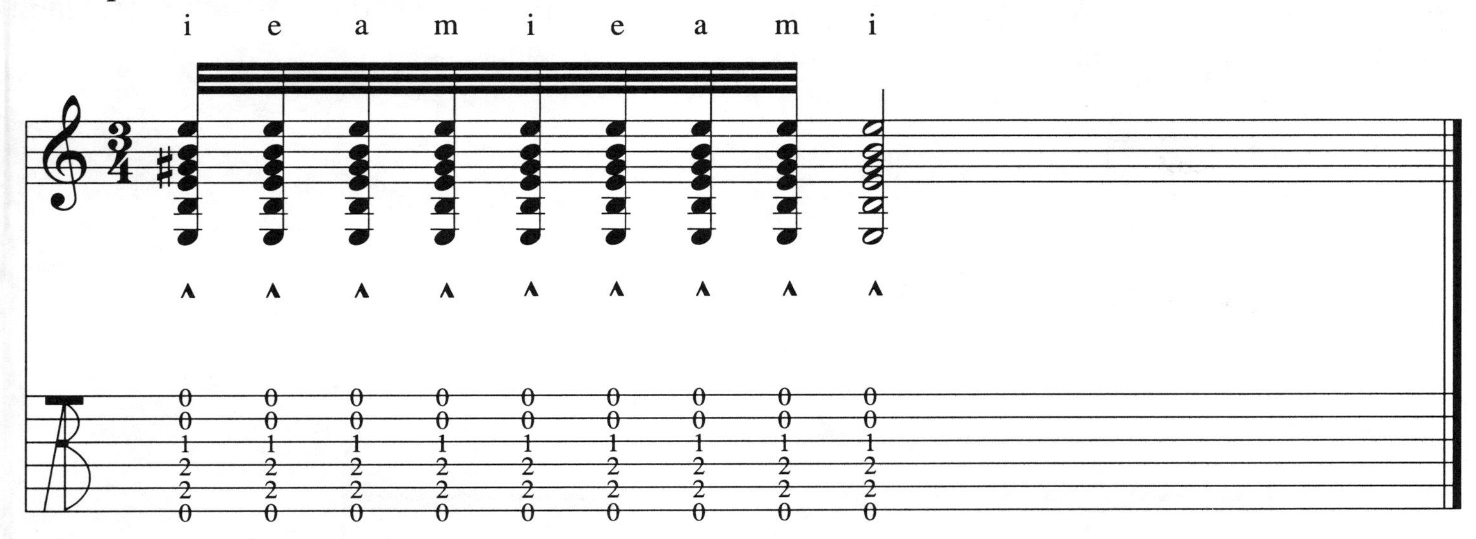

And the same idea, but with a duration of 3 beats this time;

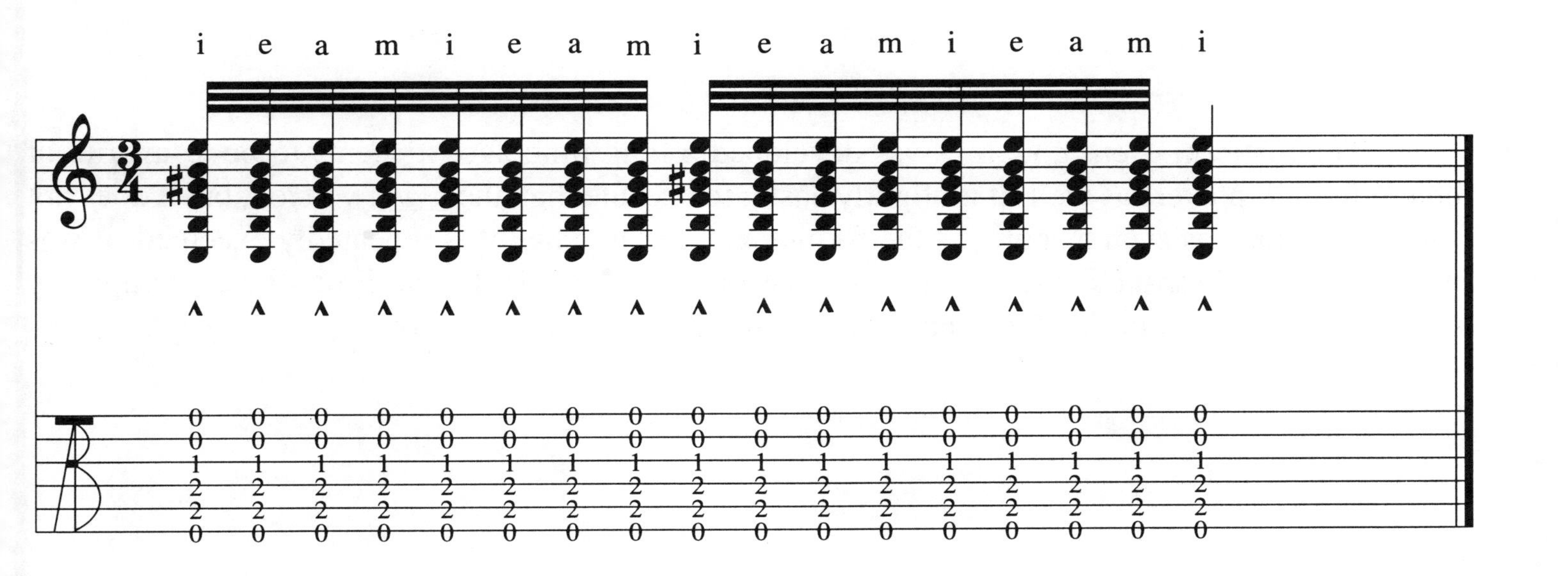

The **amii** rasgueado:

This variation starts with the ring finger, omitting the little finger and compensates by adding an upstroke with the index at the end of the beat:

Movement description: This is executed as a stream of continuous 16th notes; out of each group of four notes the ring finger plays the first, the middle finger plays the 2nd, the index finger plays the 3rd and the index finger plays again, but with an upstroke this time, the 4th note. Hand position is the same as in the basic rasgueado.

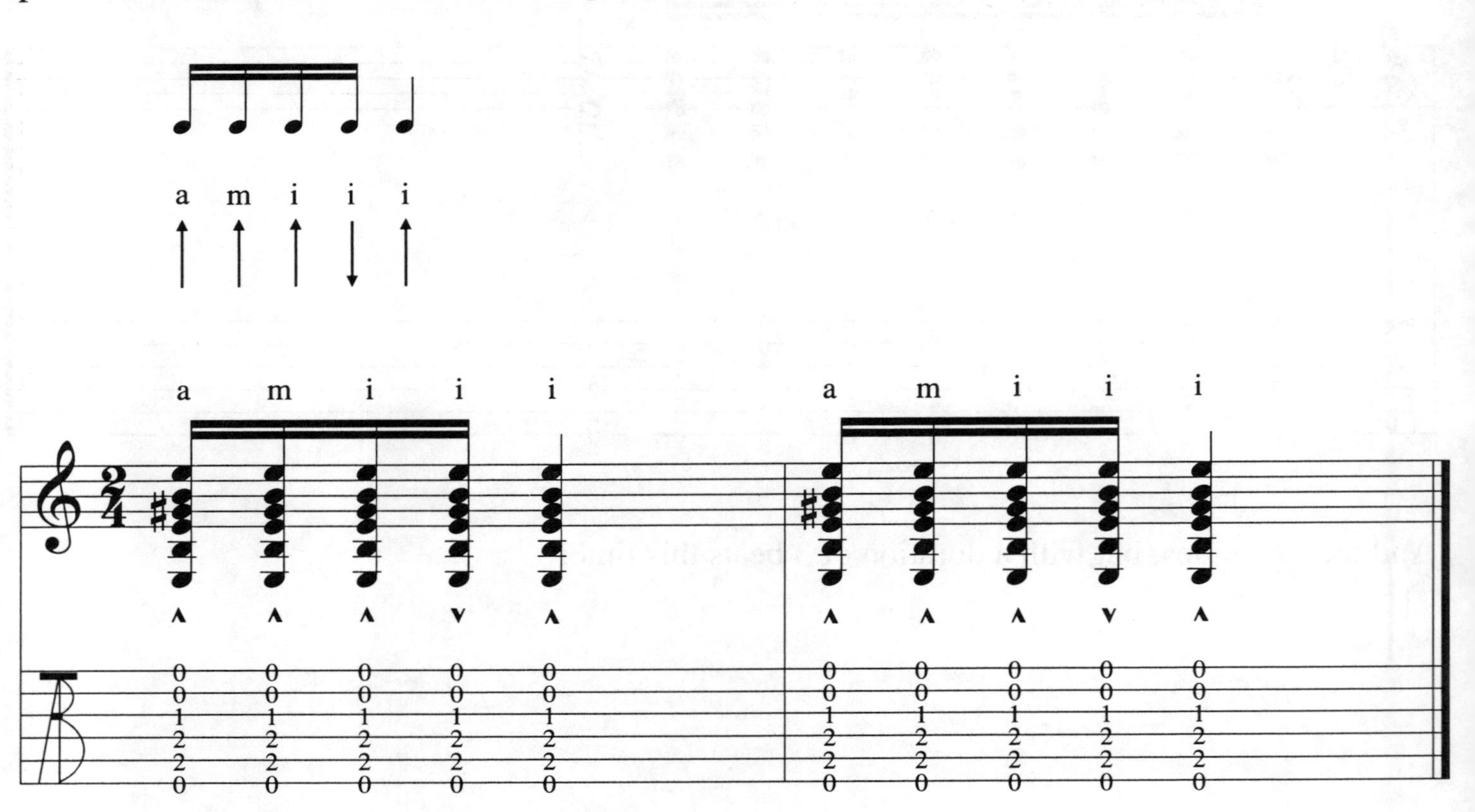

This pattern, even though it was developed a long time ago, it seems to be a favorite of contemporary players as well. It is slightly easier to execute than the *ieami* version, but it does not usually produce as even a sound as the former, especially when it is repeatedly executed. It was widely used by Mario Escudero, Diego del Gastor and Perico del Lunar. From the contemporary players, I've seen Gerardo Nunez and Moraito use this form extensively.

Here's an example in the form of Soleares, where this pattern is used continuously:

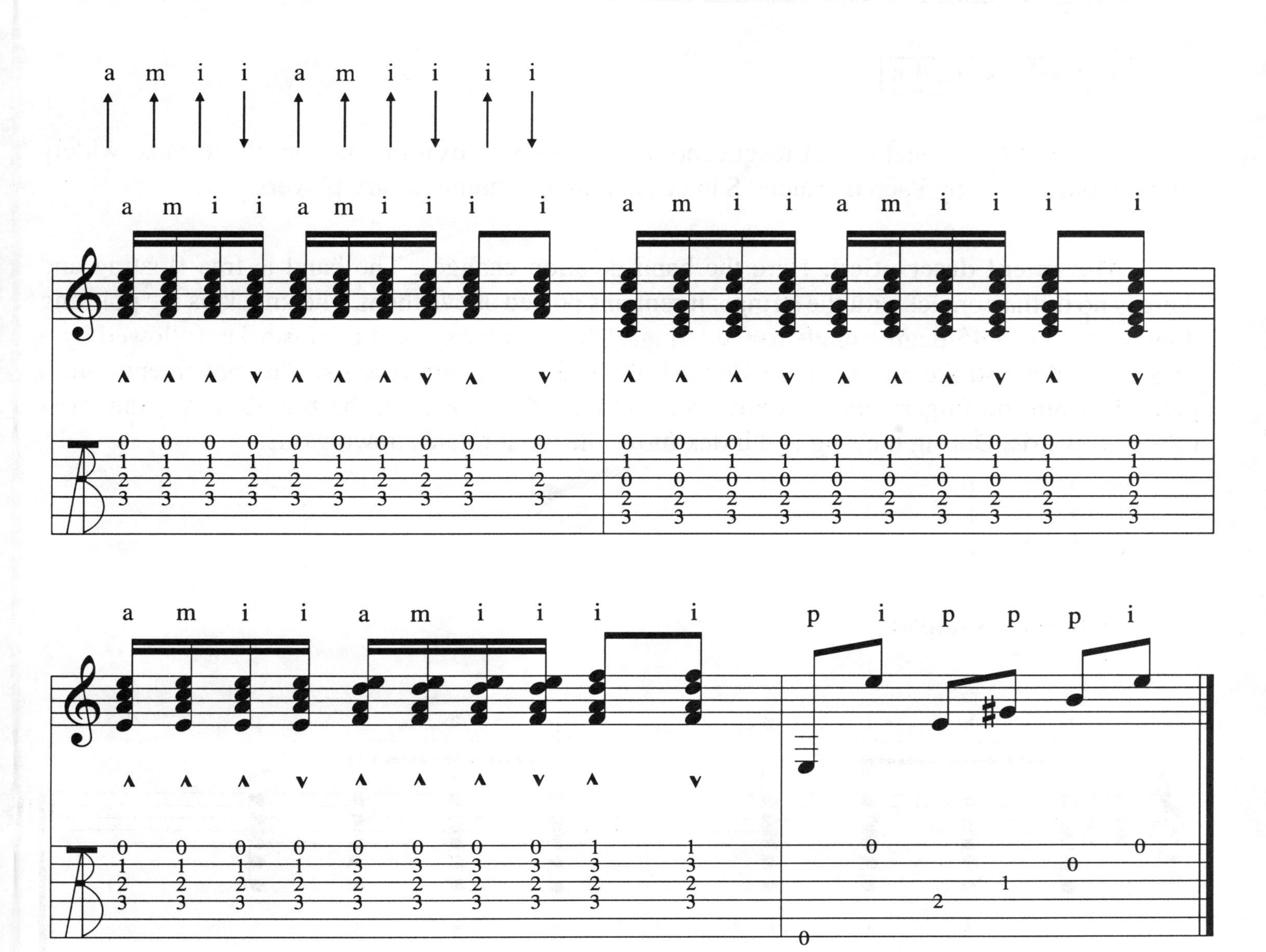

Triplet & Sextuplet traditional rasgueados

The **pai** rasgueado:

The first traditional triplet rasgueado pattern we will examine is one of the most widely adopted ones, used by Paco de Lucia, Sabicas and many contemporary players.

Movement description: Here the hand position changes. The hand is free floating and there is no initial contact with the strings; it remains poised above them. The knuckles are pointing downwards, on a 45-degree angle to the strings. The thumb executes an upstroke, followed by a ring finger downstroke and an index downstroke and the pattern repeats. The movement comes partially from the fingers and partially from rotating the wrist. On the thumb move, the wrist rotates upwards. During the ring and index move the wrist rotates downwards.

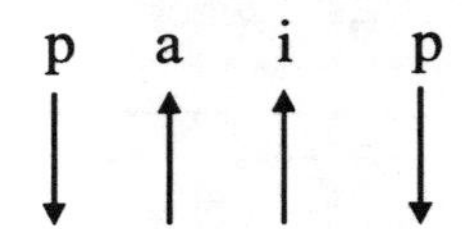

Here's an example:

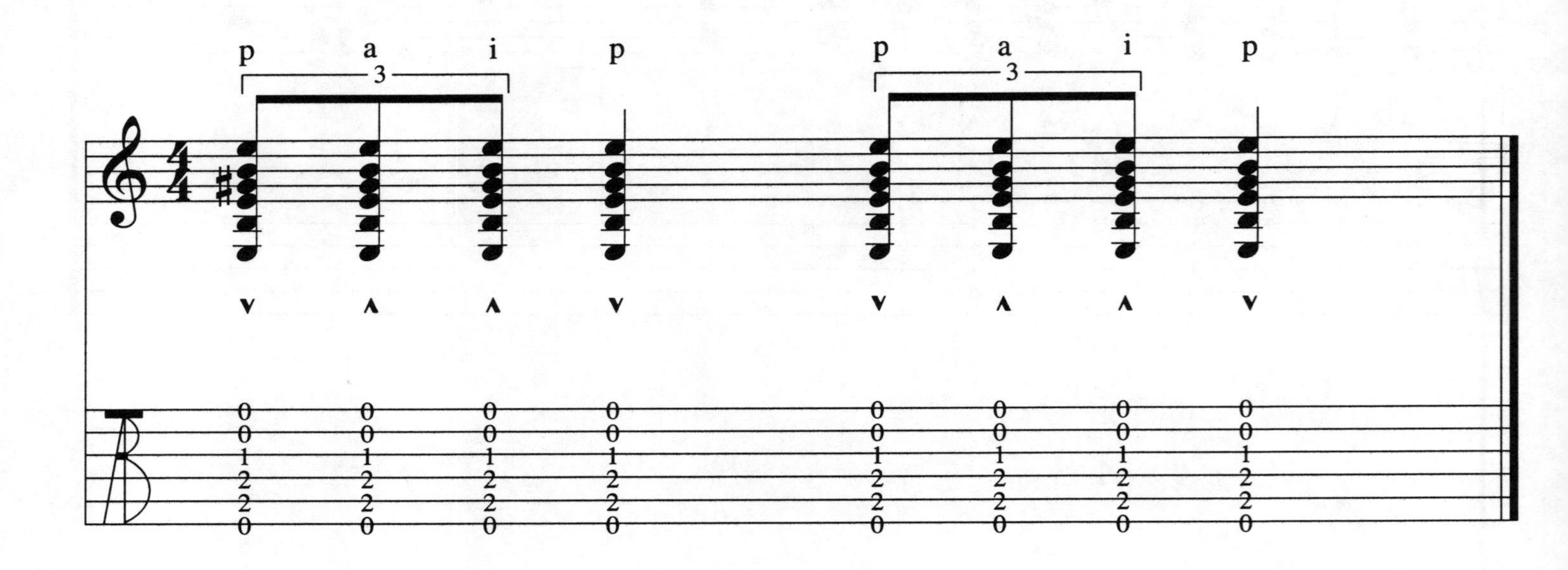

This pattern can be used to play triplets, sextuplets and even 32nd note triplets! Here's an example of an ending **por Bulerias** using this rasgueado form, in triplets:

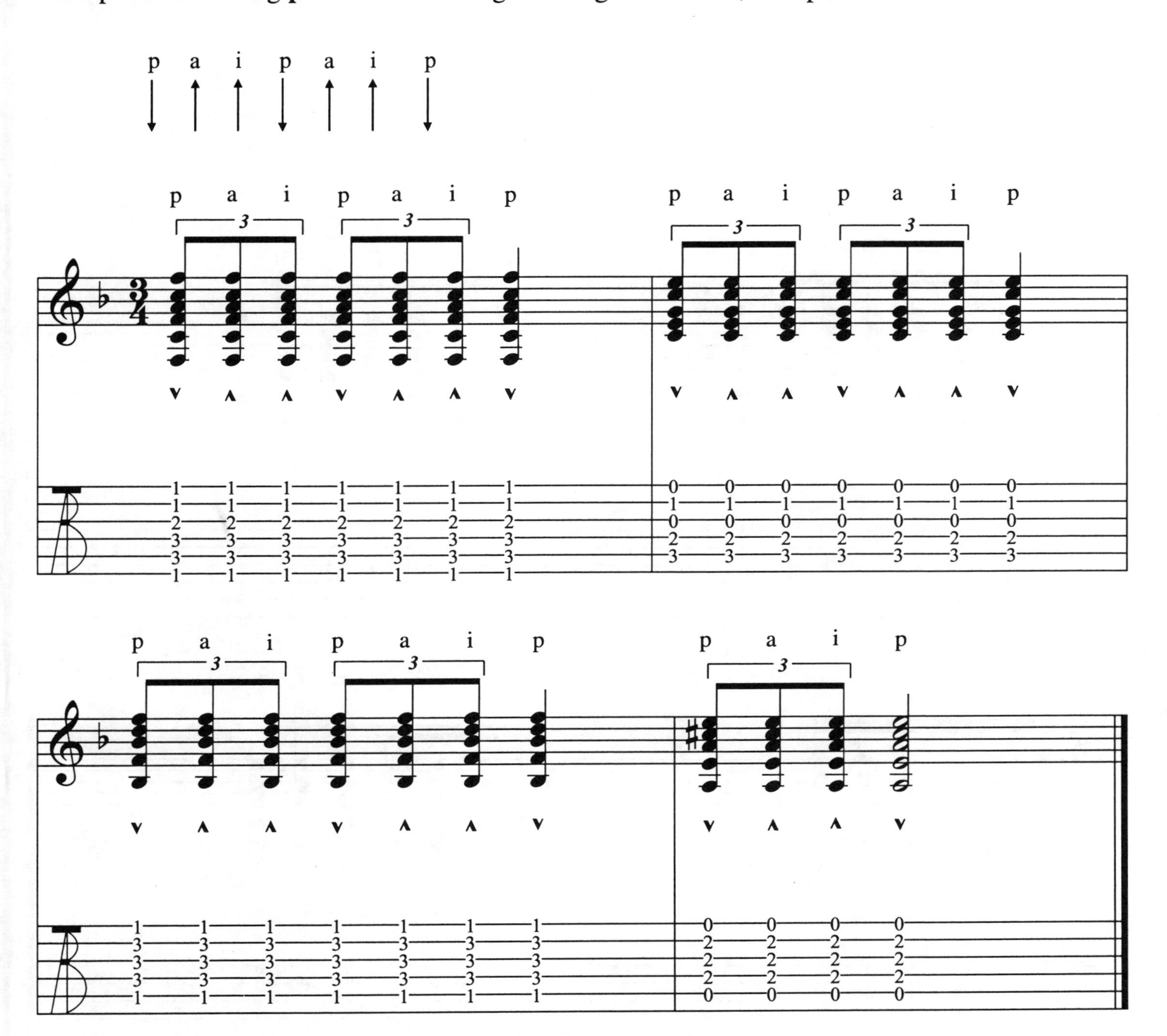

Here's another example, in sextuplets this time.

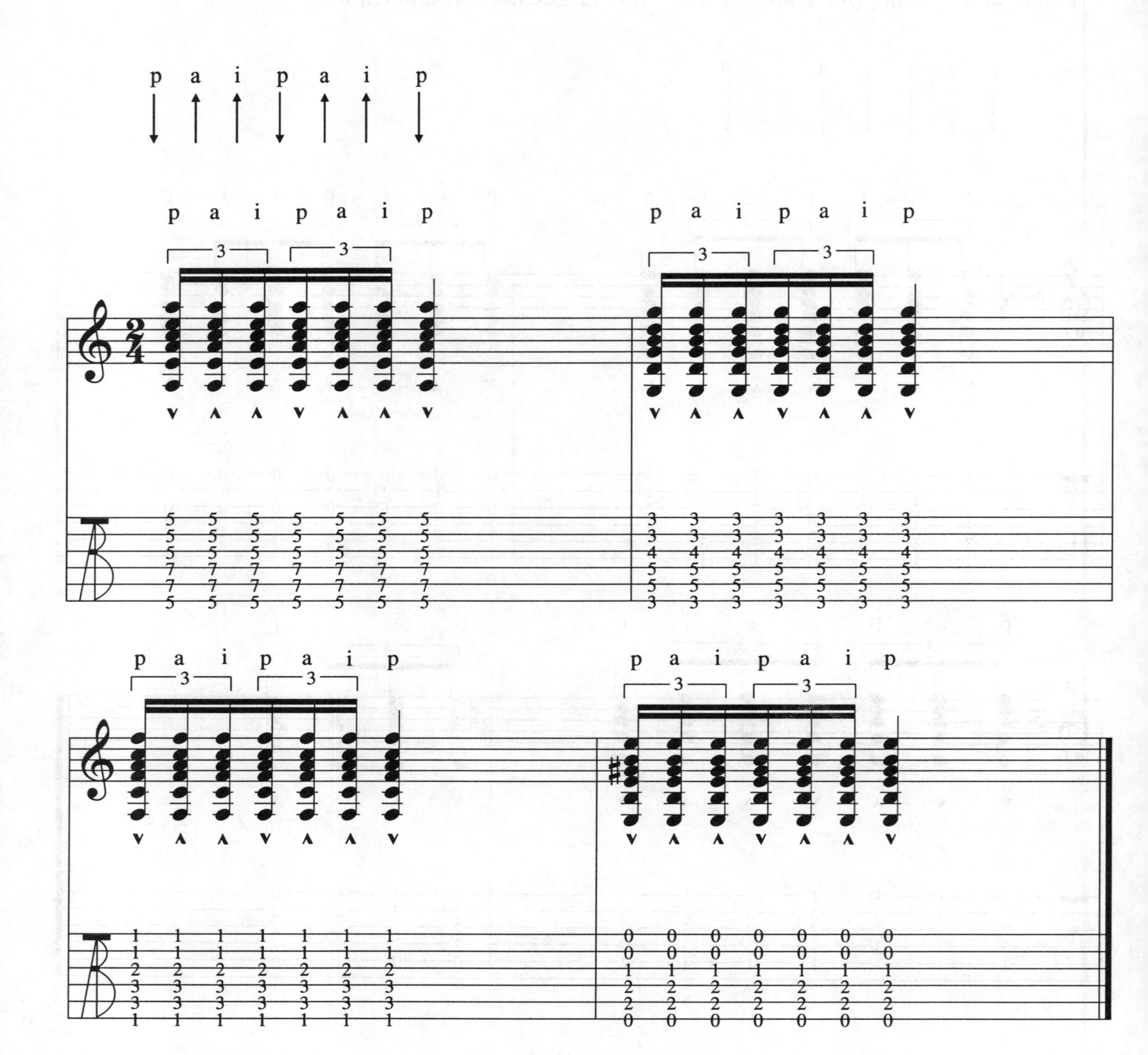

The **pei** rasgueado:

This variation is the same as the previous pattern, with only the little finger being used in the place of the ring finger. Paco Pena showed it to me, and, as he pointed out, it relies slightly more on individual finger movement than wrist rotation. The triplet feel seems to be a little more understated in this version, compared with the *pai* pattern.

Movement description: Once more, the hand is free floating and there is no continuous contact to the strings; The knuckles are pointing downwards, on a 30 degree angle to the strings, to compensate for the smaller length of the little finger. The thumb executes an upstroke, followed by a little finger downstroke and an index downstroke and the pattern repeats. The movement comes partially from the fingers and partially from rotating the wrist. On the thumb move, the wrist rotates upwards. During the little and index move the wrist rotates downwards.

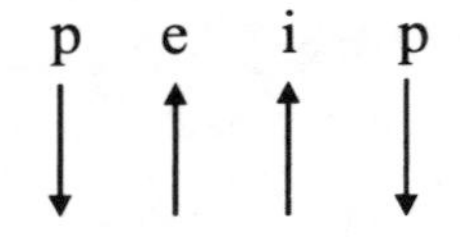

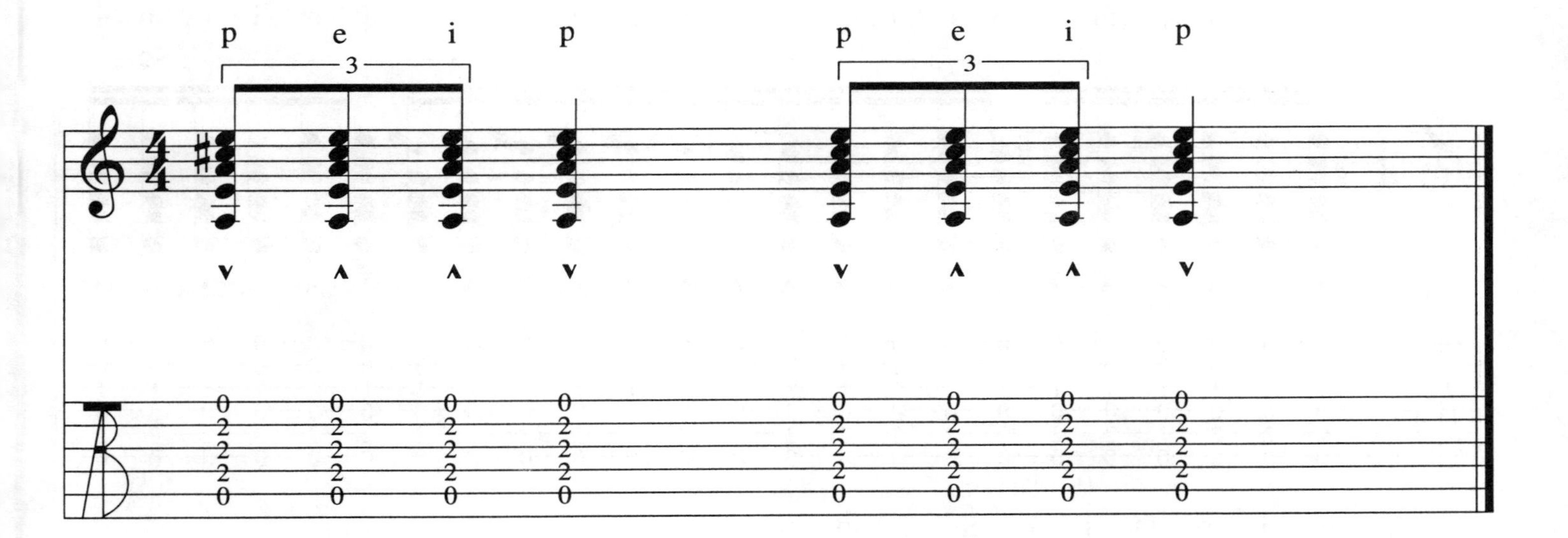

The **pmi** rasgueado:

The final variation on the *pai* pattern, this form is exactly the same as the previous one, only the middle finger is used in place of the little finger. Popularized by the great concertista Serranito in the late '60s, it produces a smooth waterfall effect and is not very rhythmically pronounced. Another incredible flamenco guitarist, Sabicas, also used this pattern.

Movement description: Once more, the hand is free floating and there is no continuous contact with the strings; the knuckles are pointing downwards, on a 45-degree angle to the strings. The thumb executes an upstroke, followed by a middle finger downstroke and an index downstroke and the pattern repeats. The movement comes partially from the fingers and partially from rotating the wrist. On the thumb move, the wrist rotates upwards. During the little and index move the wrist rotates downwards.

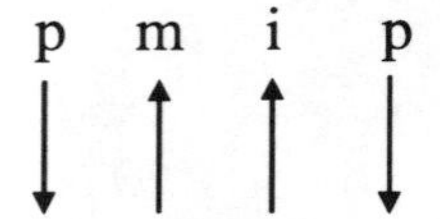

Here's an example based on the Farucca form;

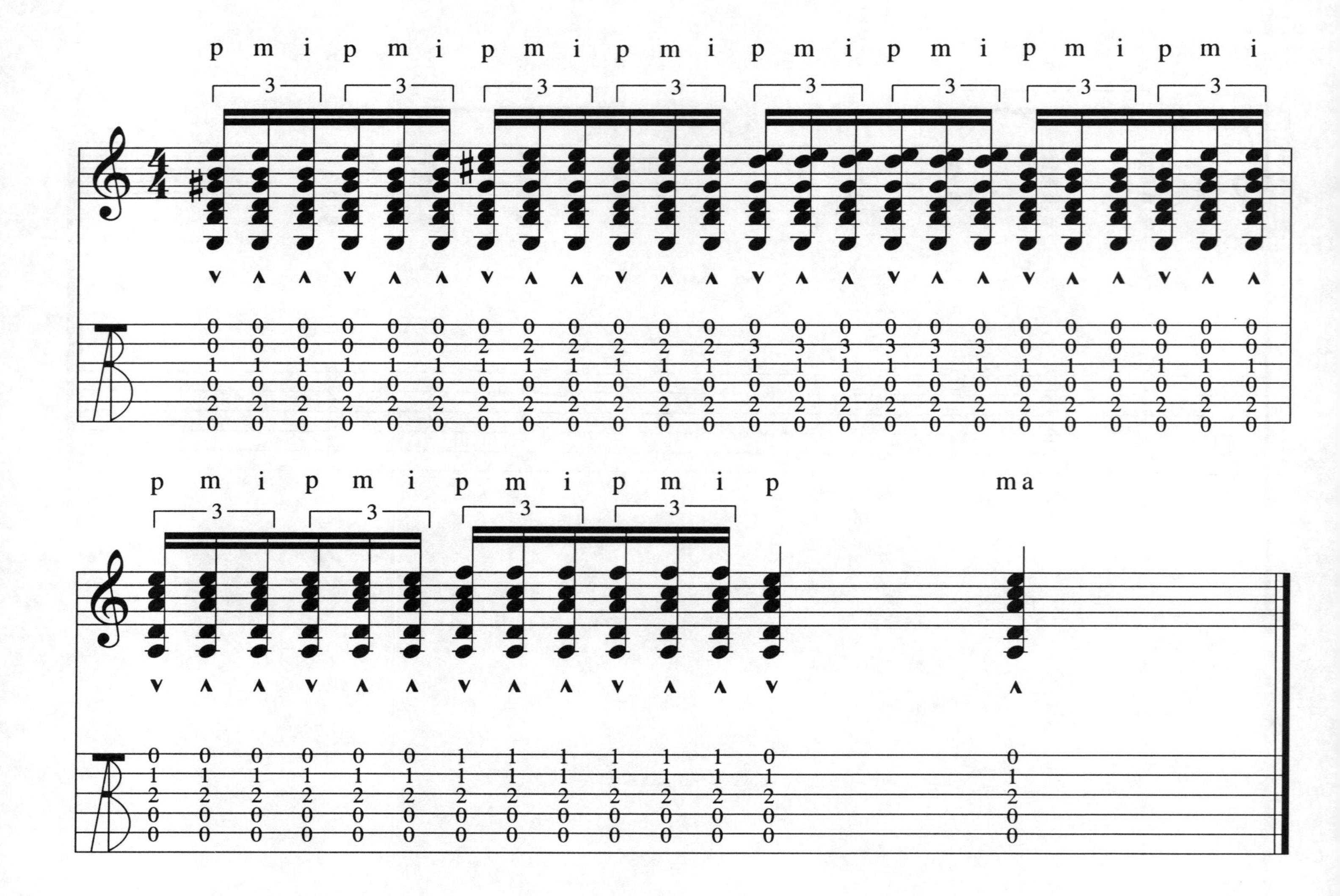

The **pmp** rasgueado:

This traditional triplet rasgueado is comprised of a thumb upstroke, a middle finger downstroke and a thumb downstroke.

Movement description: Once more, the hand is free floating and there is no continuous contact with the strings; the knuckles are pointing downwards, on a 45-degree angle to the strings. The thumb executes an upstroke, followed by a middle finger downstroke and a thumb downstroke and the pattern repeats. The movement comes partially from the fingers and partially from rotating the wrist. On the thumb upstroke, the wrist rotates upwards. During the middle downstroke and the thumb downstroke the wrist rotates downwards.

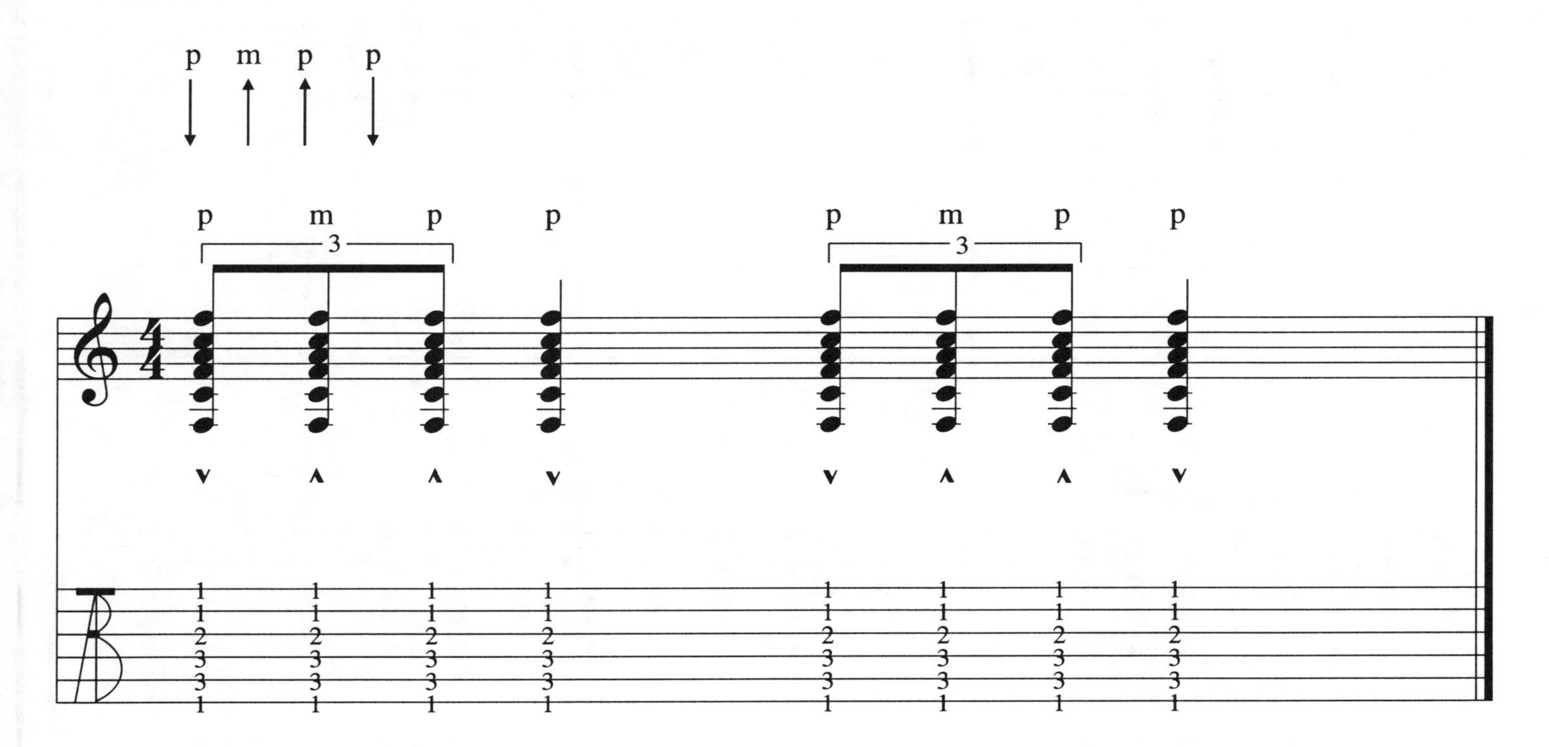

This is a louder, very rhythmic rasgueado, that is widely used when accompanying dance. Not really known for its dynamic subtlety, it can nevertheless be heard under the most adverse conditions. It is a favorite of Juan Martin.

Here's an ending for a Rumba in Em, using this rasgueado in sextuplets:

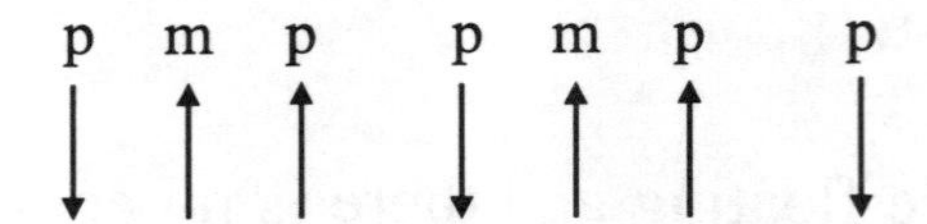

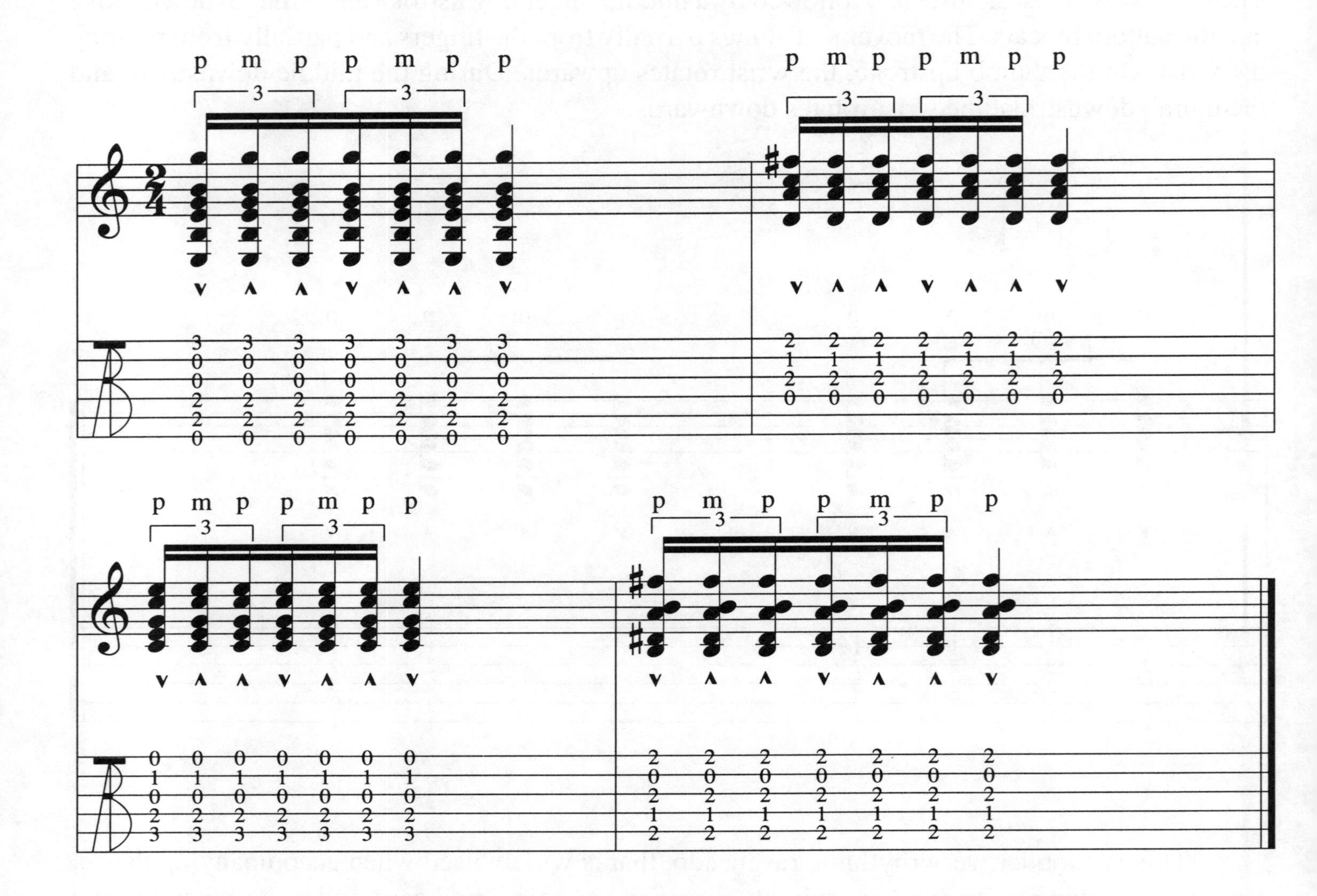

Gypsy Kings, the French rumba masters use this rasgueado in practically all their fast paced pieces.

Quintuplet traditional rasgueados

Another rhythmic subdivision widely used in the medium tempo flamenco forms is the 5-notes-per-beat or quintuplet rasgueado. There are situations when the tempo is too slow to make triplets or 16th notes effective, but too fast to allow sextuplets or 32nd notes and in these cases the quintuplet rasgueados are used.

The **eamii** rasgueado:

This is a variation of the basic rasgueado pattern, adding one index upstroke at the end of the pattern.

Movement description: This is played usually as a stream of continuous quintuplets. Out of each group of five notes the little finger plays the 1st, the ring finger plays the 2nd , the middle finger plays the 3rd , the index finger plays the 4th, and the index finger plays again, but with an upstroke this time, the 5th note. Hand position is the same as in the basic rasgueado.

Here's a 2-beat example played on a static E major chord:

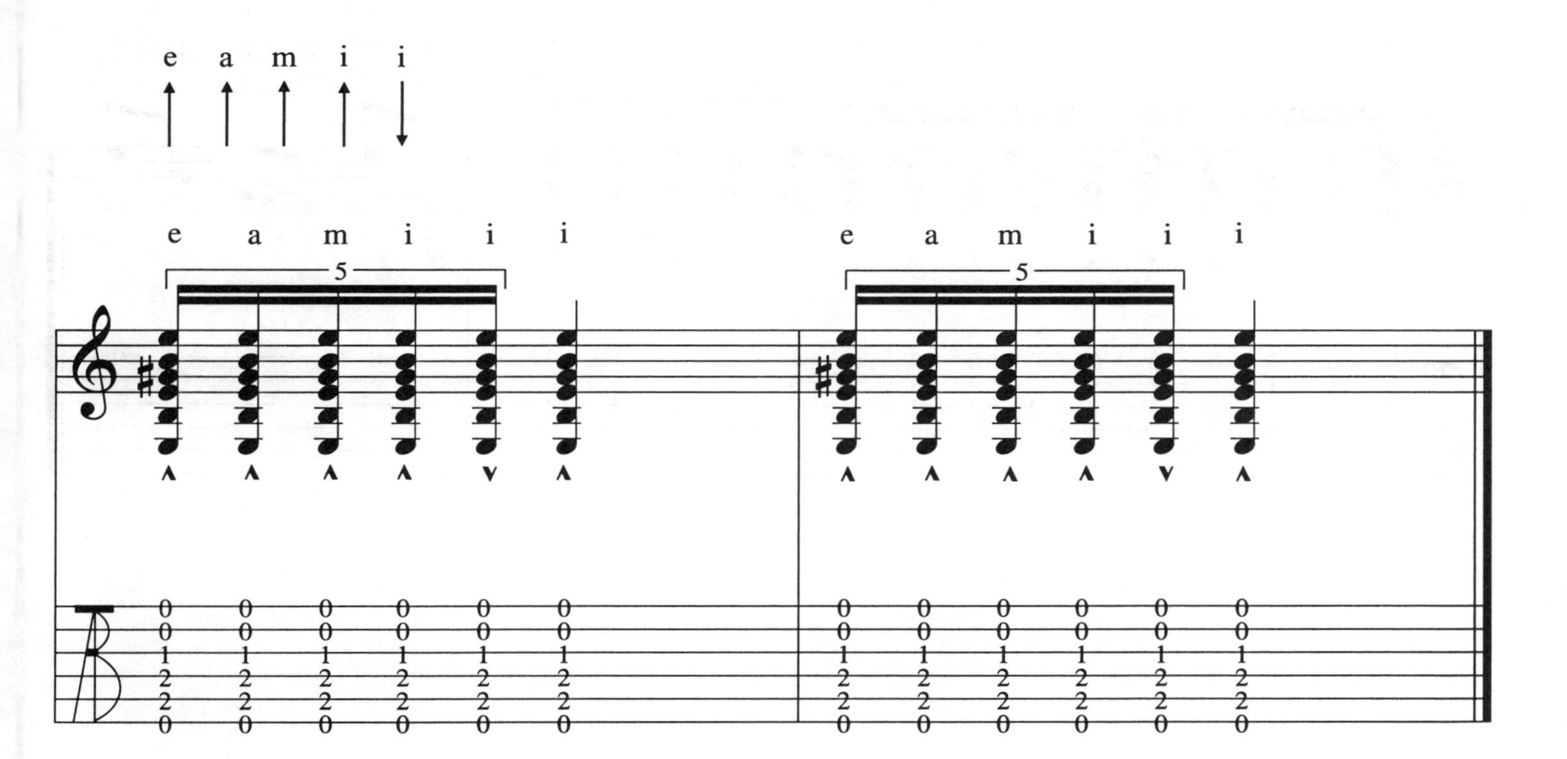

This pattern was a favorite of Sabicas; he also used it as a continuous roll, in order to create a "waterfall" effect. It was shown to me by Juan Martin. Here's the example, in the form of Soleares that Juan Martin used when demonstrating the pattern:

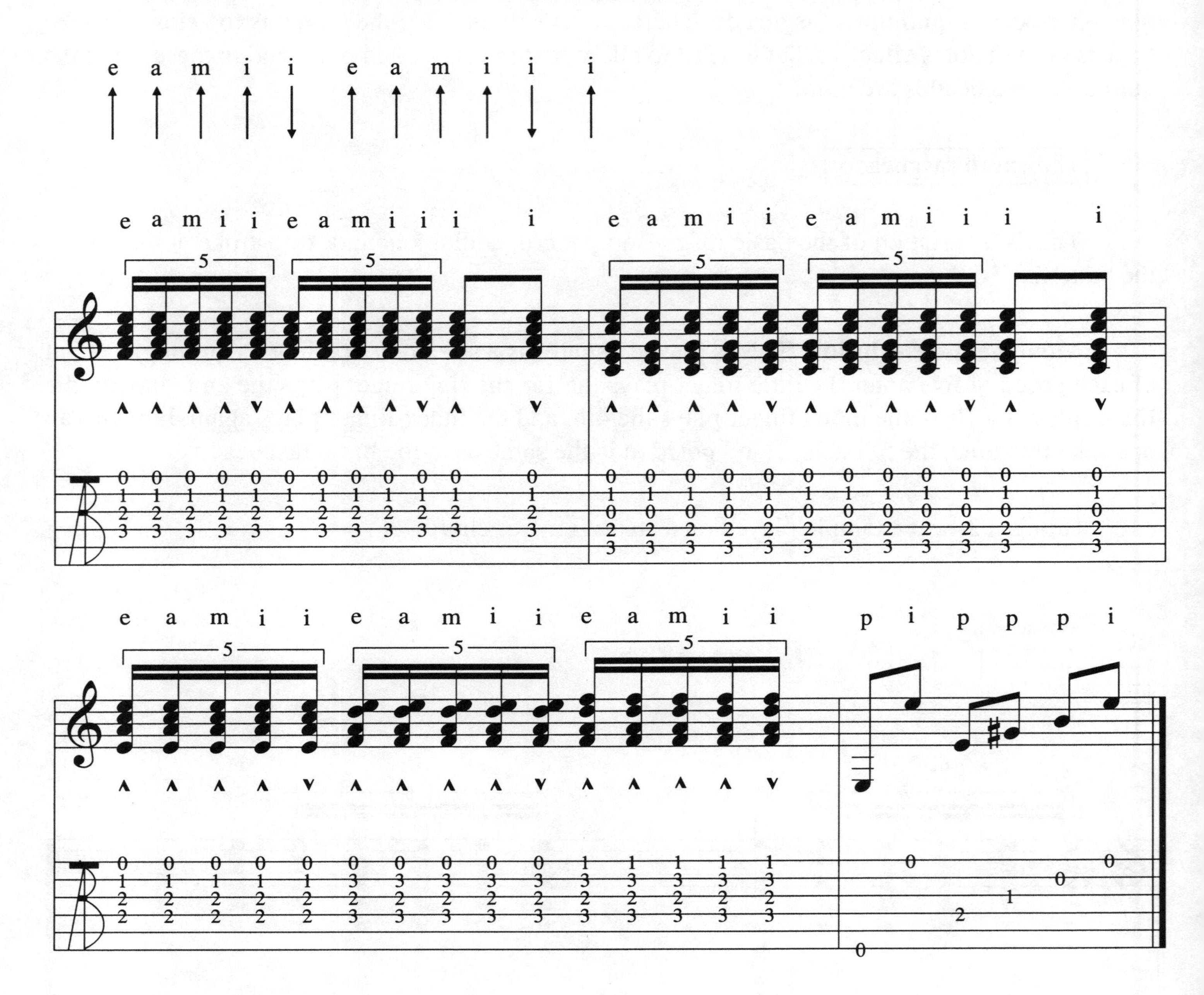

Here's an introduction to an Alegrias in Em by the great Sabicas, using the same pattern:

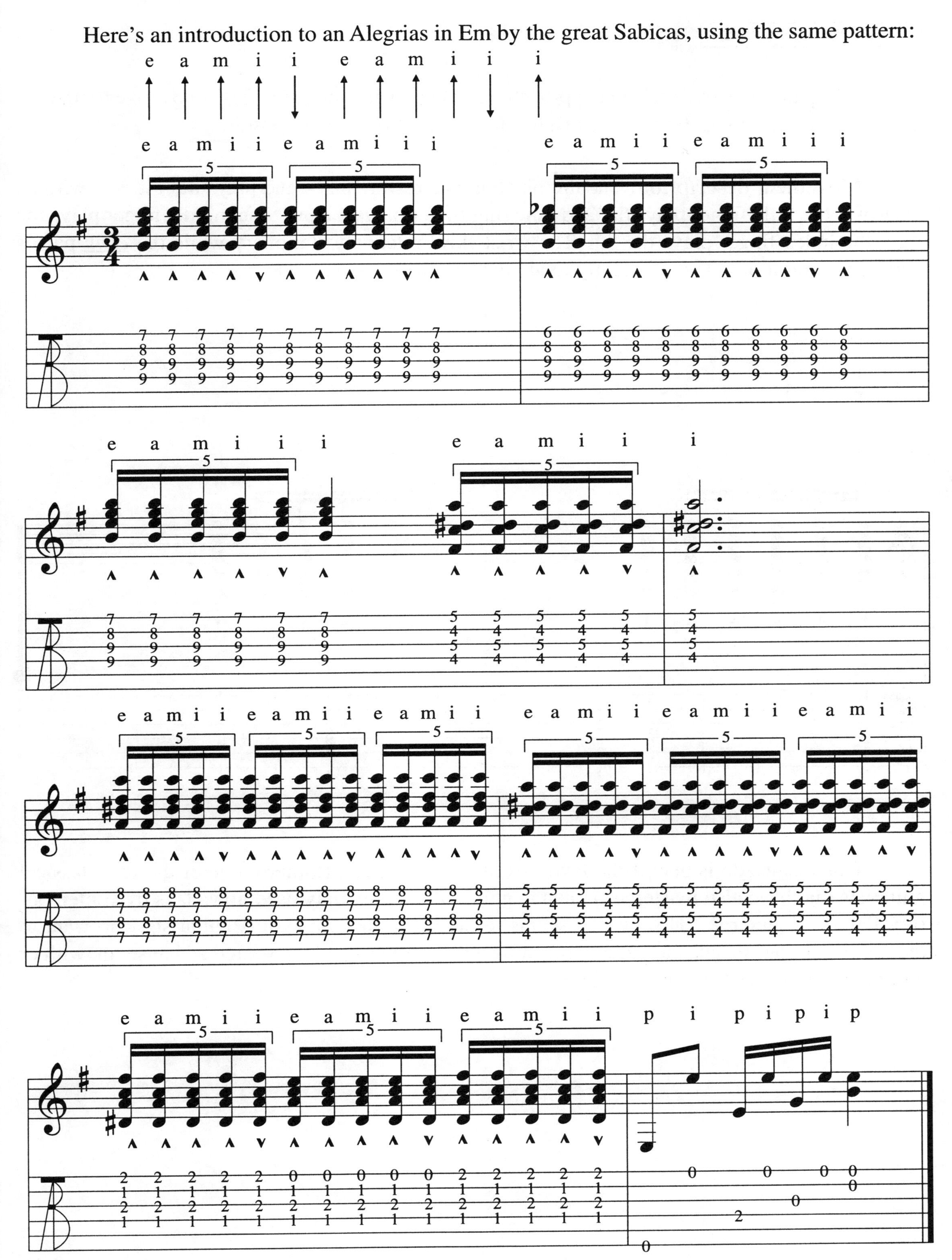

The **peami** rasgueado:

This pattern takes a different approach; instead of using the index finger upstroke for the 5th note, it uses a thumb upstroke. This rasgueado uses the "free" hand position.

Movement description: The thumb aborts its resting place and plays the 1st note with an upstroke, the little finger plays the 2nd , the ring finger plays the 3rd , the middle finger plays the 4th , the index finger plays the 5th. The wrist stays relatively stationary while the eami part is performed and it only moves slightly to aid the thumb on its upstroke:

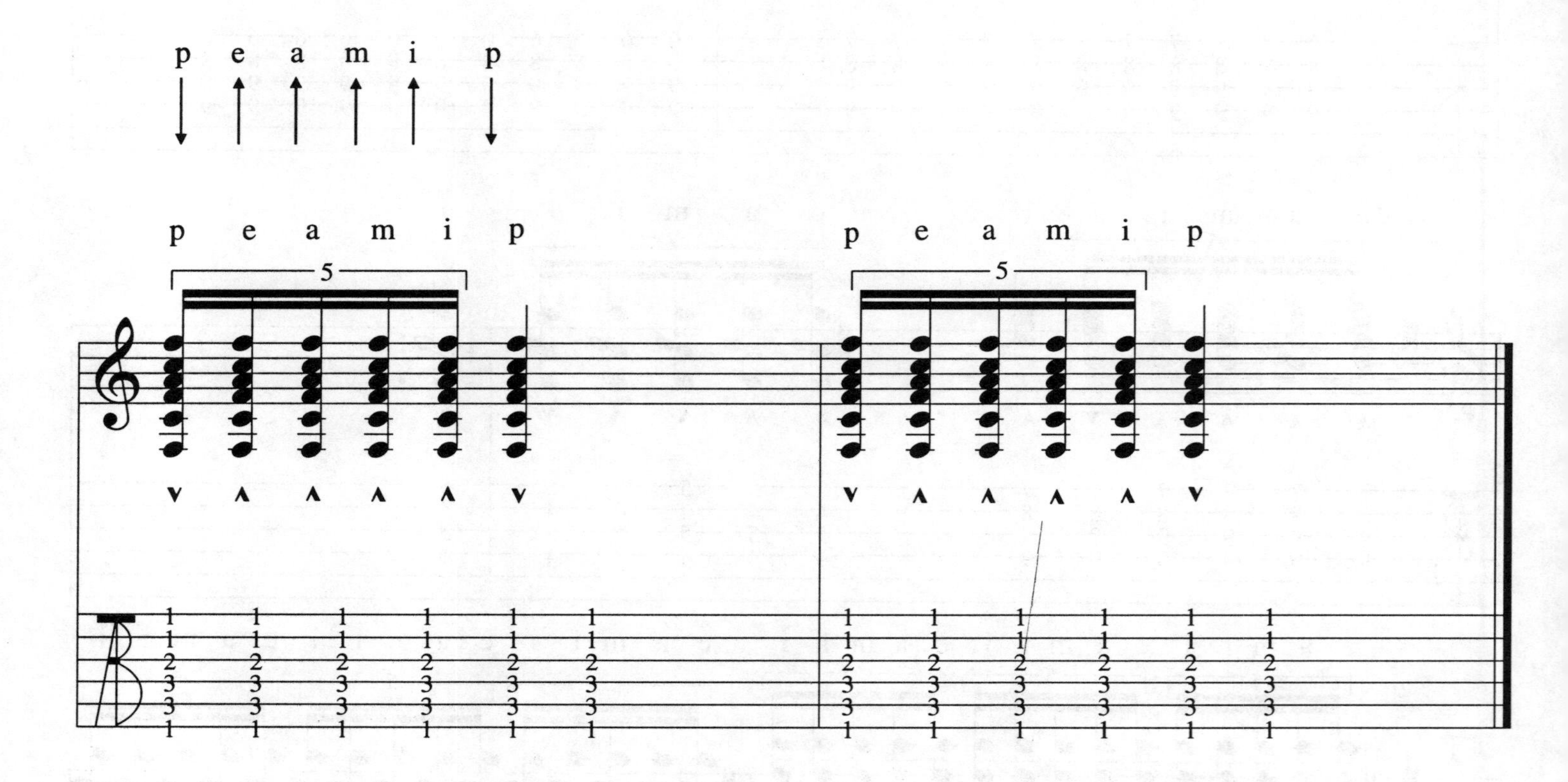

This rasgueado is one of the favorites of the great Pepe Romero, one of the few classical guitarists that have also mastered flamenco guitar. It is not widely used nowadays by contemporary flamenco guitarists. However, it seems to be a favorite of classical guitarists who want to learn a continuous rasgueado pattern, meaning a pattern that can be repeated ad nauseum, with or without specific strict rhythmic structure.

Contemporary Rasgueados

The patterns that will follow are very useful and will invariably add great impact and spice to your playing, but require almost extreme care when following the description, because one false stroke direction will ensure failure. So, be very careful and thorough when first reading the description of each pattern. Since the majority of the rasgueados from now on can be used in different rhythmic settings, in many cases I will refrain from putting them into specific categories of rhythmic subdivisions, opting instead to offer more elaborate examples demonstrating their versatility and usefulness.

Triplet rasgueados

The **iai** rasgueado:

Movement Description: The thumb rests lightly on the 6th string. The other RH fingers, especially the ring finger, are loosely curled in the palm in a very relaxed way. Then the index plays an upstroke, followed by a ring downstroke and finally, an index finger downstroke.

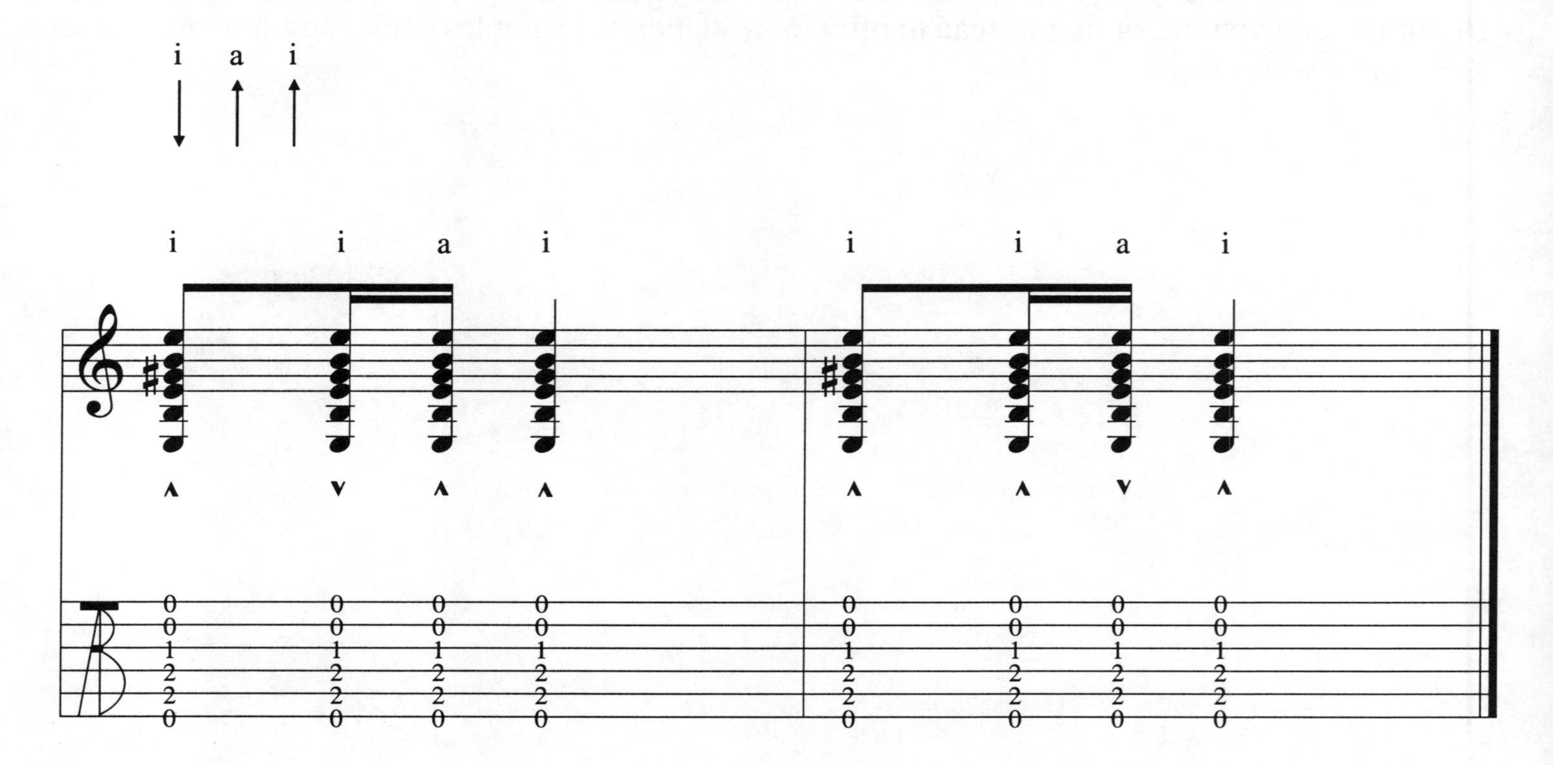

This is probably the most widely used pattern for triplets; virtually all contemporary players play triplets this way most of the time. I learned this pattern from Moraito Chico, the son of the great traditional flamenco guitarist, Moraito. When practiced adequately, this pattern yields an extraordinarily fast triplet effect, many times reaching 32nd note triplets!

Here's an example of sextuplets based in the form of Granadina:

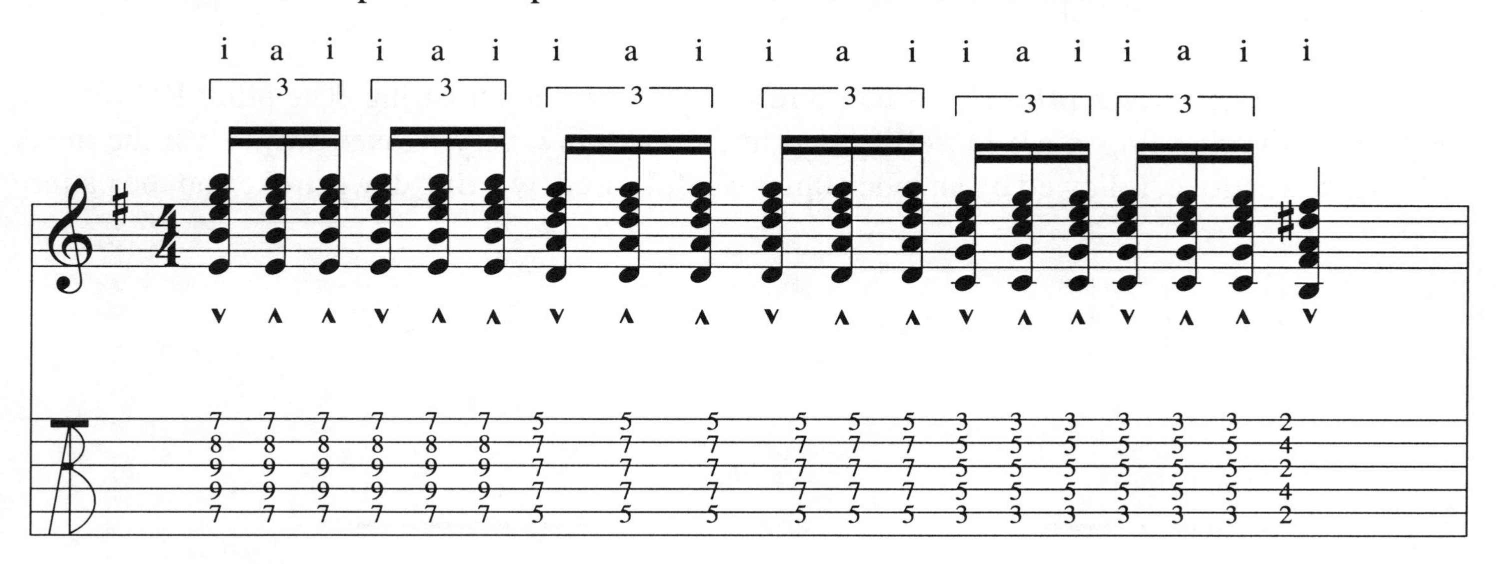

However, the same pattern can be used to play straight 16th notes in the duration of 3 beats; Here's an example in Alegrias form. This is written in the key of Em and can be used to conclude an Alegrias solo.

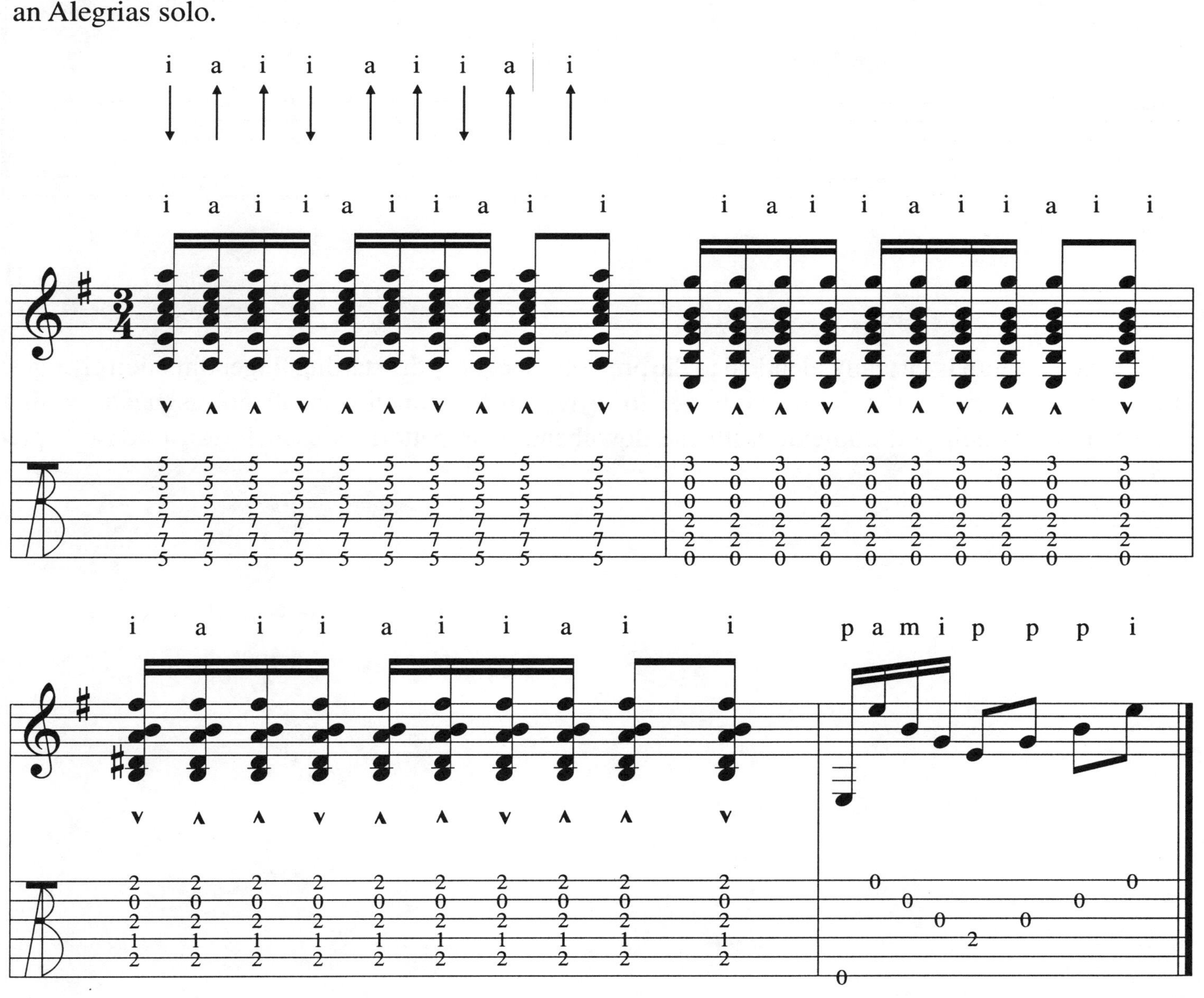

The **iia** rasgueado:

Movement description: The thumb rests lightly on the 6th string. The other RH fingers, especially the ring finger, are loosely curled in the palm in a very relaxed way. Then the index plays a downstroke, followed by an index upstroke, followed by a ring downstroke and the pattern repeats.

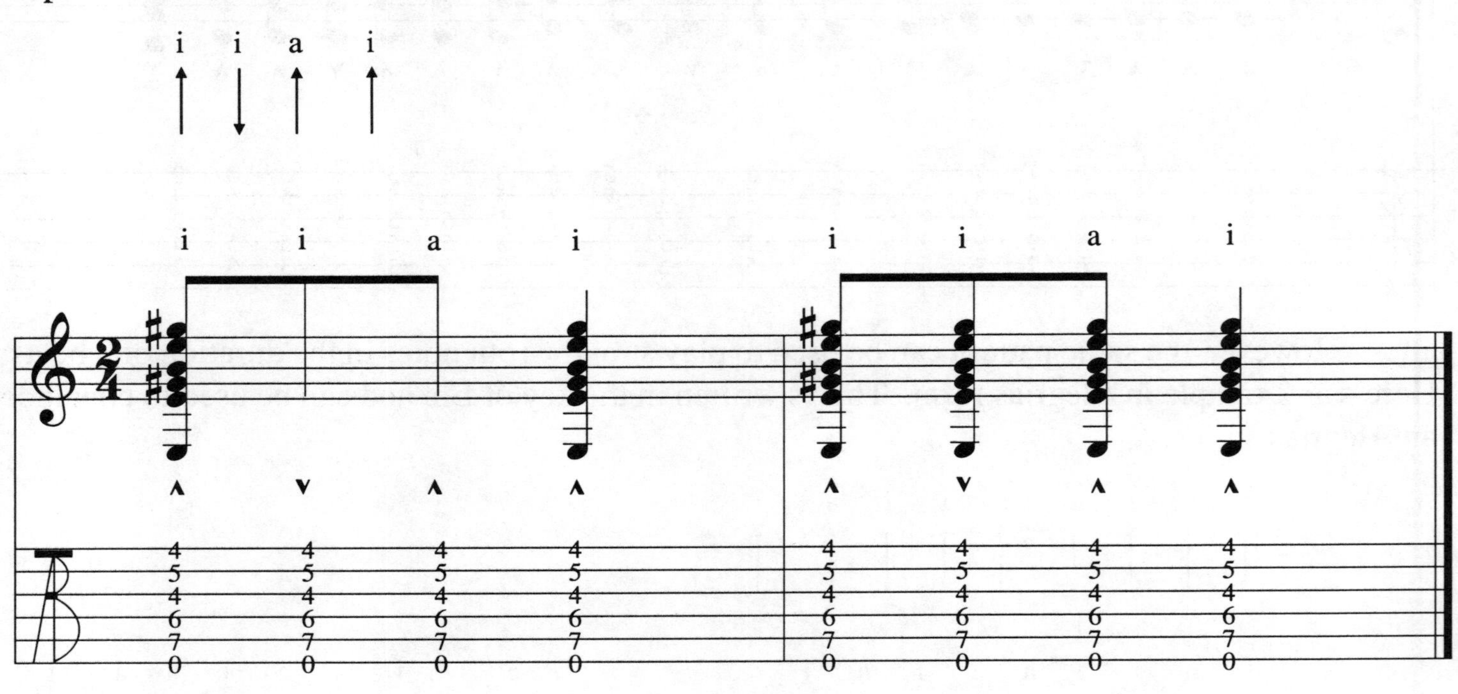

This pattern is virtually identical to the previous one; only the starting finger direction changes; this happens in order for the index finger to arrive on the conclusion of the rasgueado with a downstroke, which will coincide with the downbeat. This pattern is used for an intense triplet effect.

Here's an example by Gerardo Nunez, one of the most notable contemporary flamenco guitarists, in the form of Soleares:

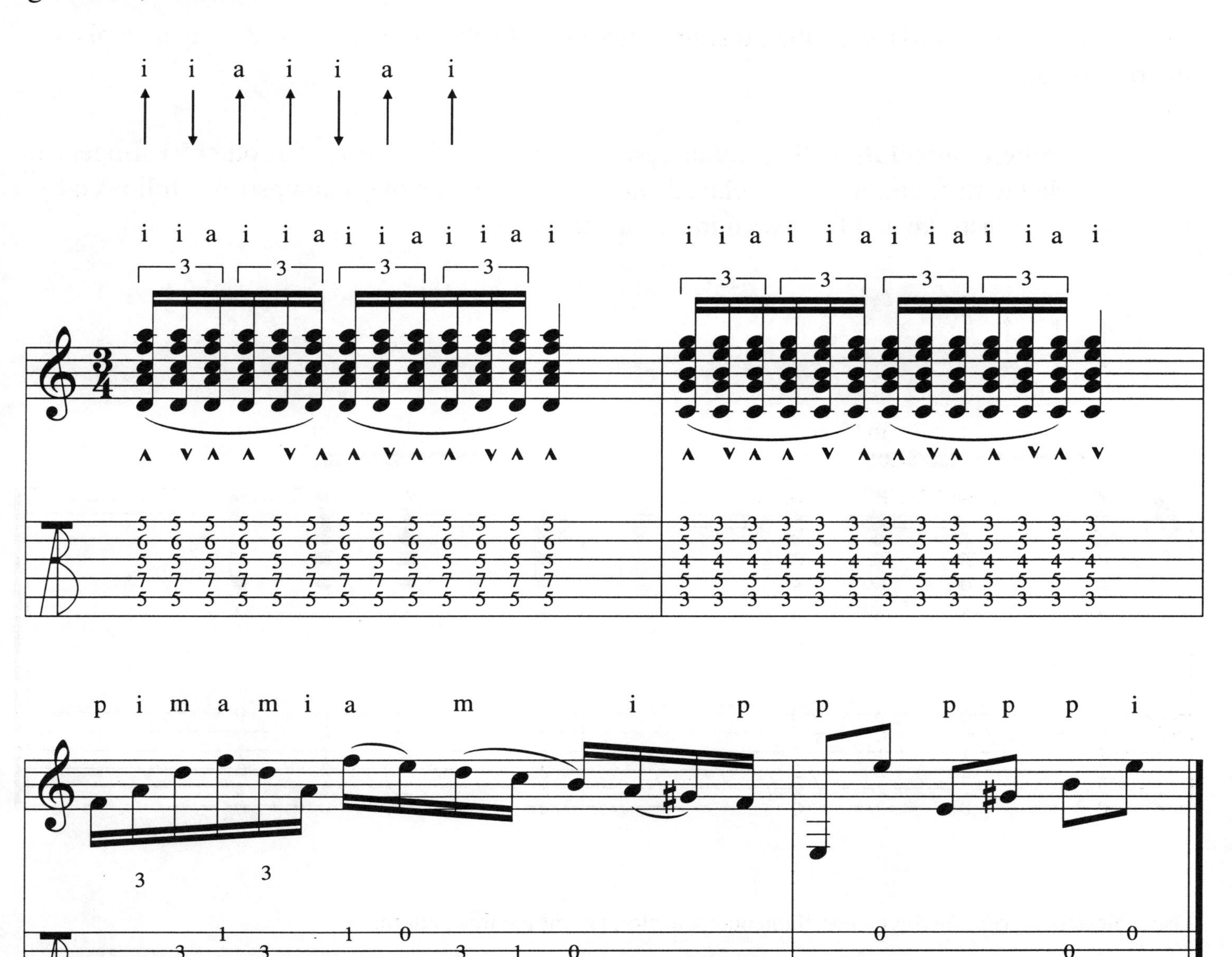

The **imi** rasgueado:

This pattern is based on the iai rasgueado, only it substitutes the middle finger in place of the ring finger.

Movement description: The thumb rests lightly on the 6th string. The other RH fingers are loosely curled in the palm in a very relaxed way. Then the index plays an upstroke, followed by a little finger downstroke and finally, an index finger downstroke.

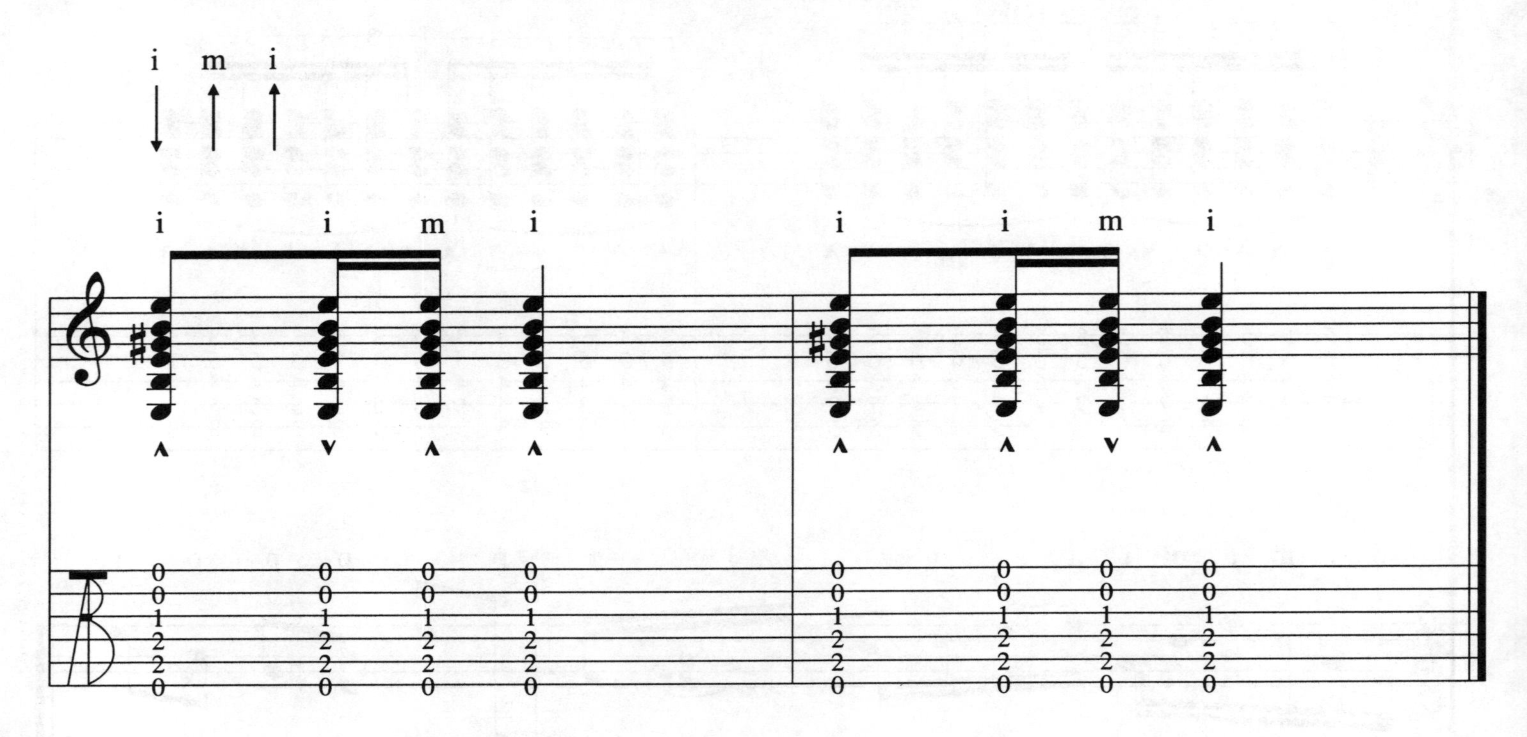

Oscar Herrero, a very distinguished flamenco educator, taught me this pattern.

The **iei** rasgueado:

This pattern is based on the *iai* rasgueado, only it substitutes the little finger in place of the ring finger.

Movement description: The thumb rests lightly on the 6th string. The other RH fingers, are loosely curled in the palm in a very relaxed way. Then the index plays an upstroke, followed by a little finger downstroke and finally, an index finger downstroke.

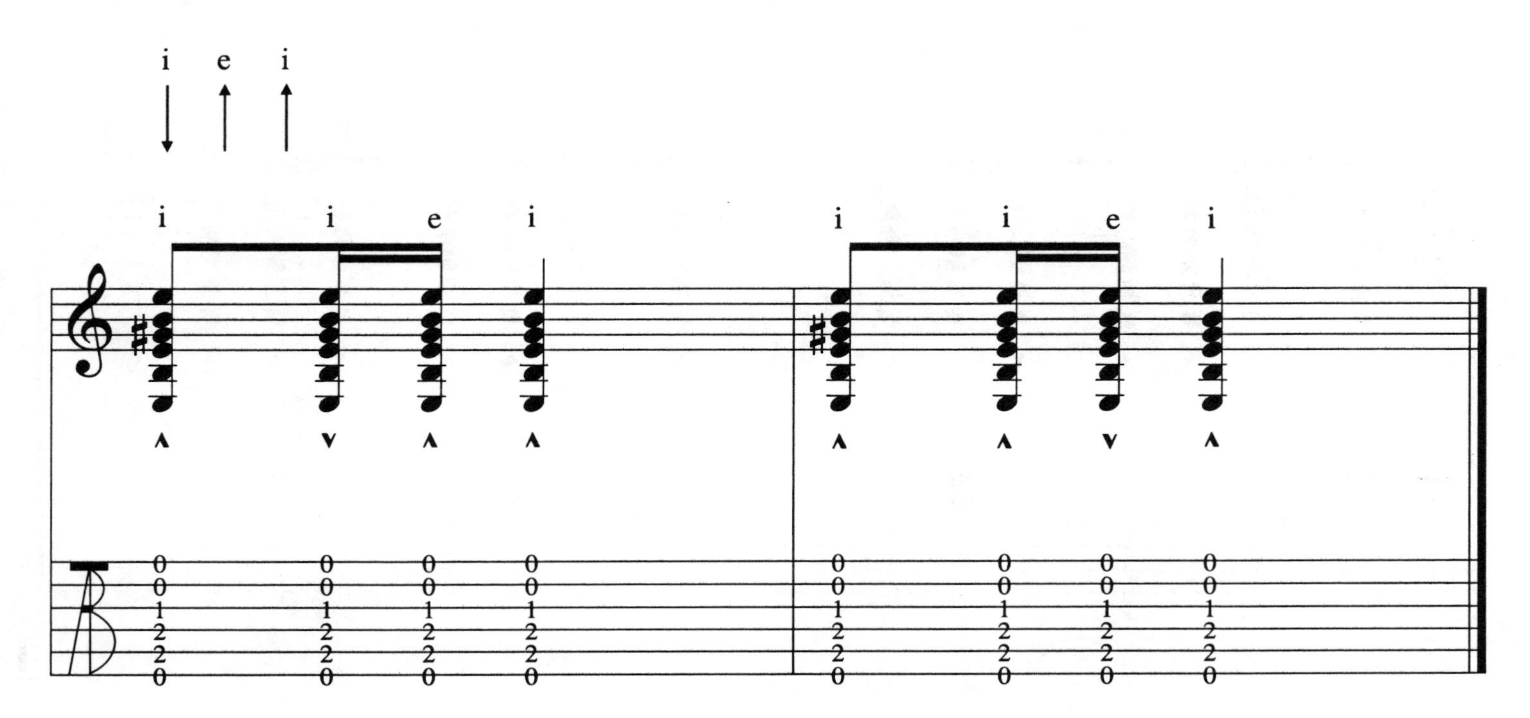

The **mmi** rasgueado:

Movement description: The thumb rests lightly on the 6th string. The other RH fingers, especially the index finger, are loosely curled in the palm in a very relaxed way. Then the middle plays an upstroke, followed by a downstroke and finally, an index finger upstroke.

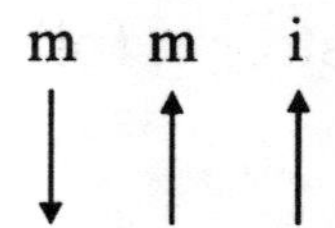

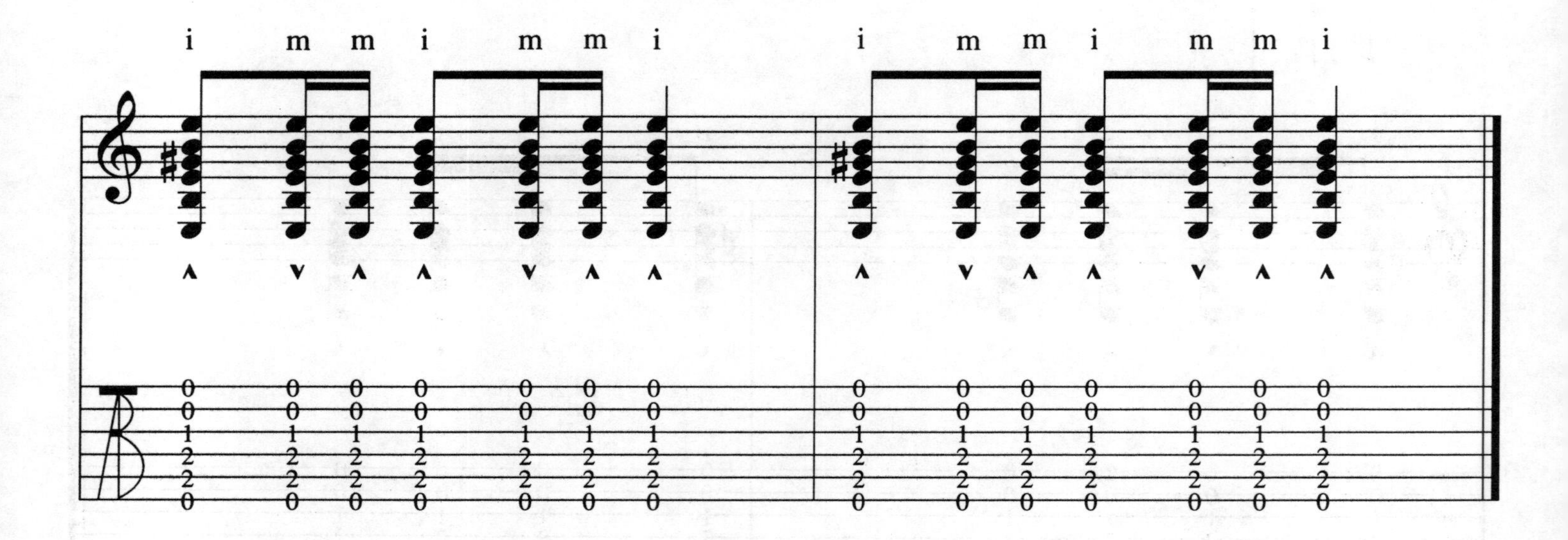

This pattern is a favorite of the great Pepe Habichuela and is considered his own innovation. Pepe also uses it frequently for 16th notes in the duration of 3 beats; Here's another example in Soleares, this time in 16th notes.

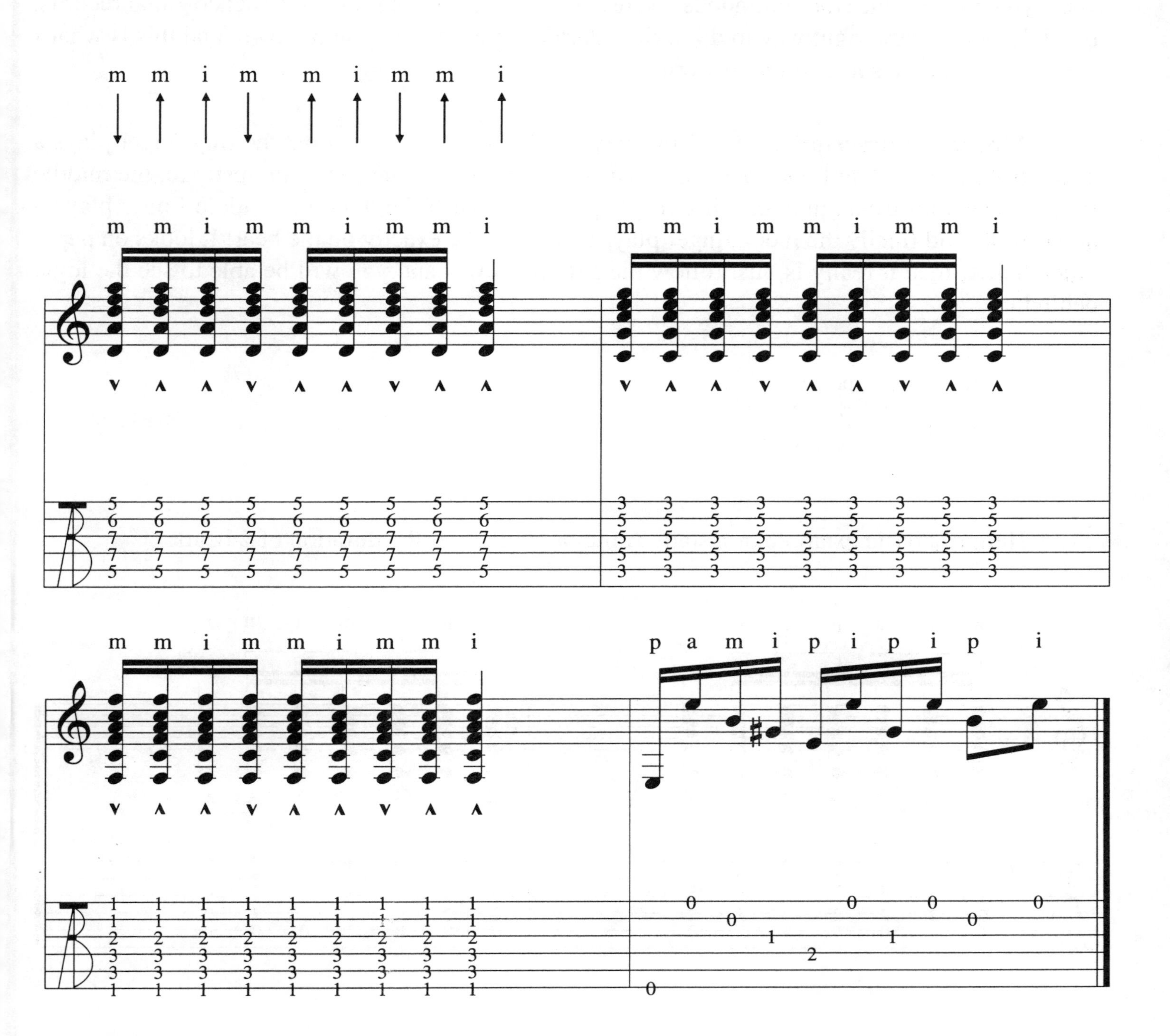

The **amamami** rasgueado:

This pattern is my own invention; I developed it by experimenting at the age of 17, when I was trying to reproduce the continuous rasgueado sounds I kept hearing on flamenco guitar records, but did not know the right way to do it. So I started experimenting on my own, and this is what I came up with; this is a sextuplet pattern:

Movement description: The hand stays in the basic position. First the ring finger plays a downstroke, the middle finger plays a downstroke, the ring finger plays an upstroke, the middle finger plays a upstroke, then the ring finger plays a downstroke, then the middle finger plays a downstroke and finally the index finger plays a downstroke exactly on the beat! It looks on paper much harder than it really is, just follow the pattern slowly and you will be able to see the logic behind it.

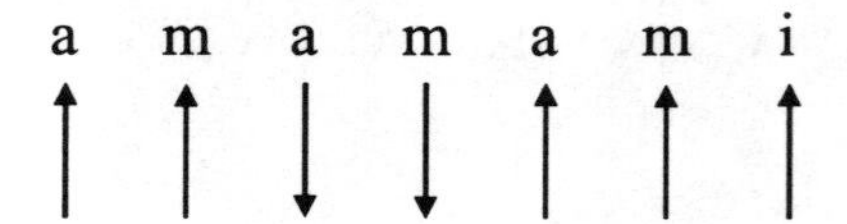

Here is a basic example of a static A major chord over the duration of 2 beats:

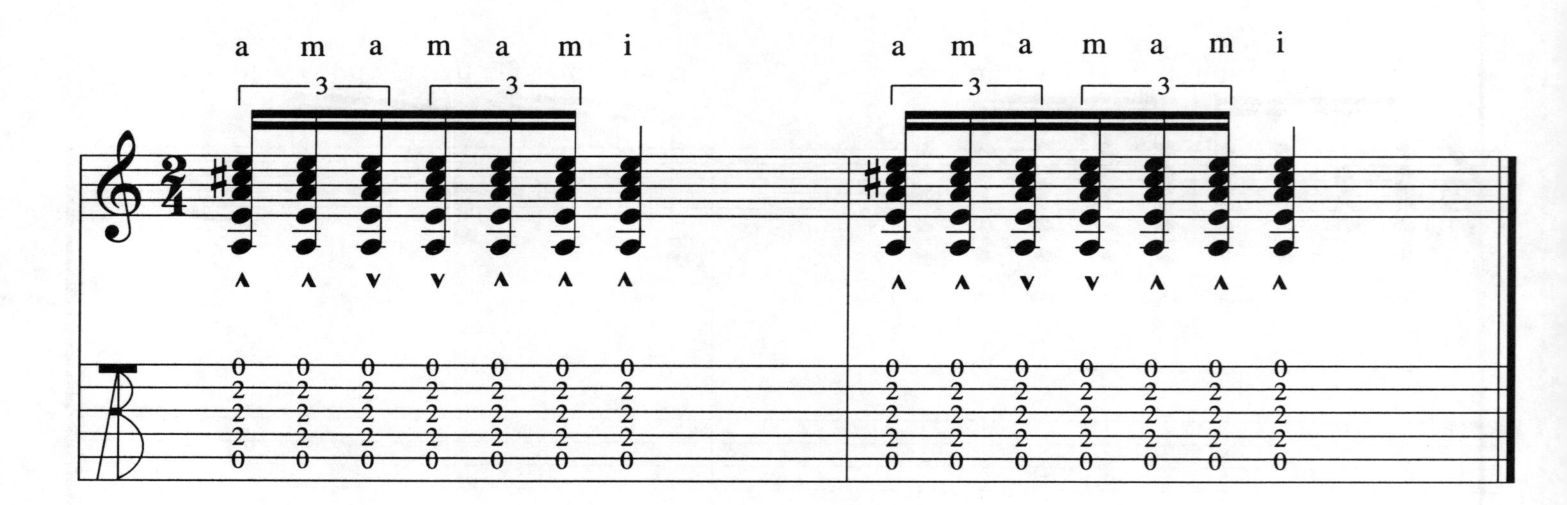

The **amamamamami** rasgueado:

The previous pattern, if repeated, will produce quintuplets over the series of 3 beats. Here's the exact pattern:

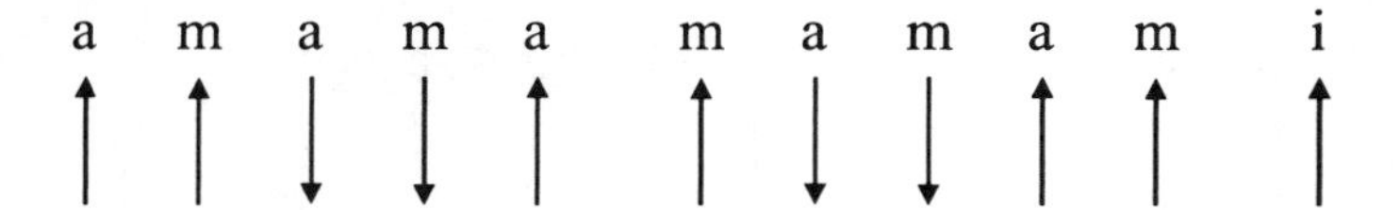

Here it is in an example in the form of Soleares:

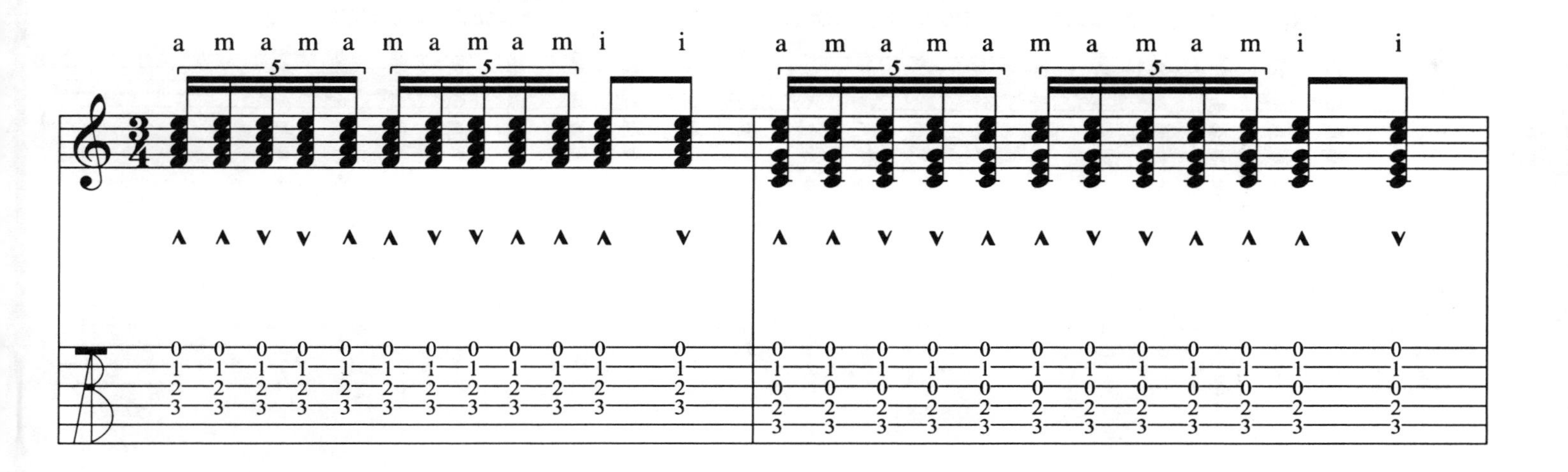

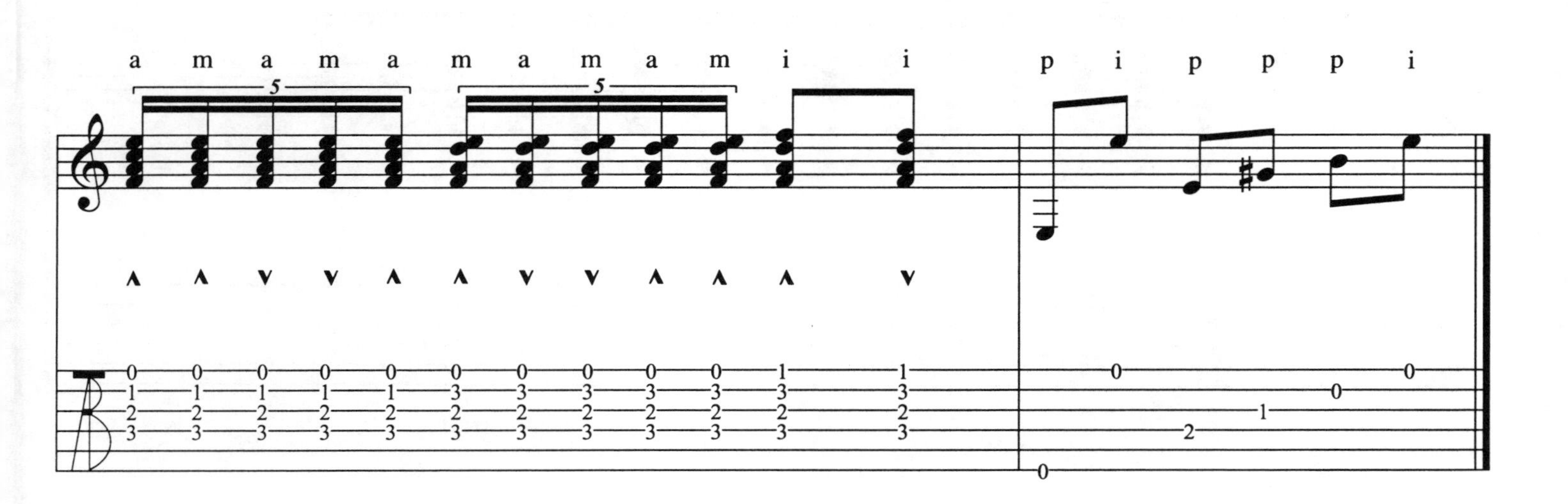

The **amamamamamamamami** rasgueado:

The very same pattern if repeated a total of three times, produces sextuplets that have duration of 4 beats; here's an example based on the form of Farucca

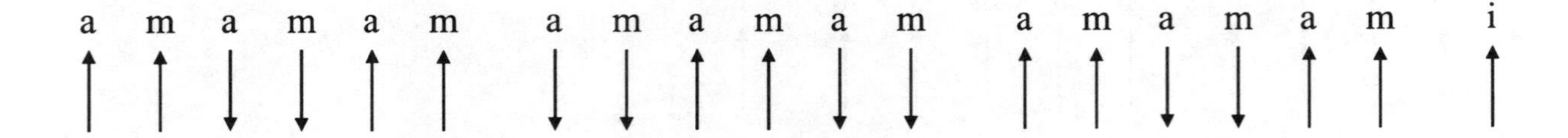

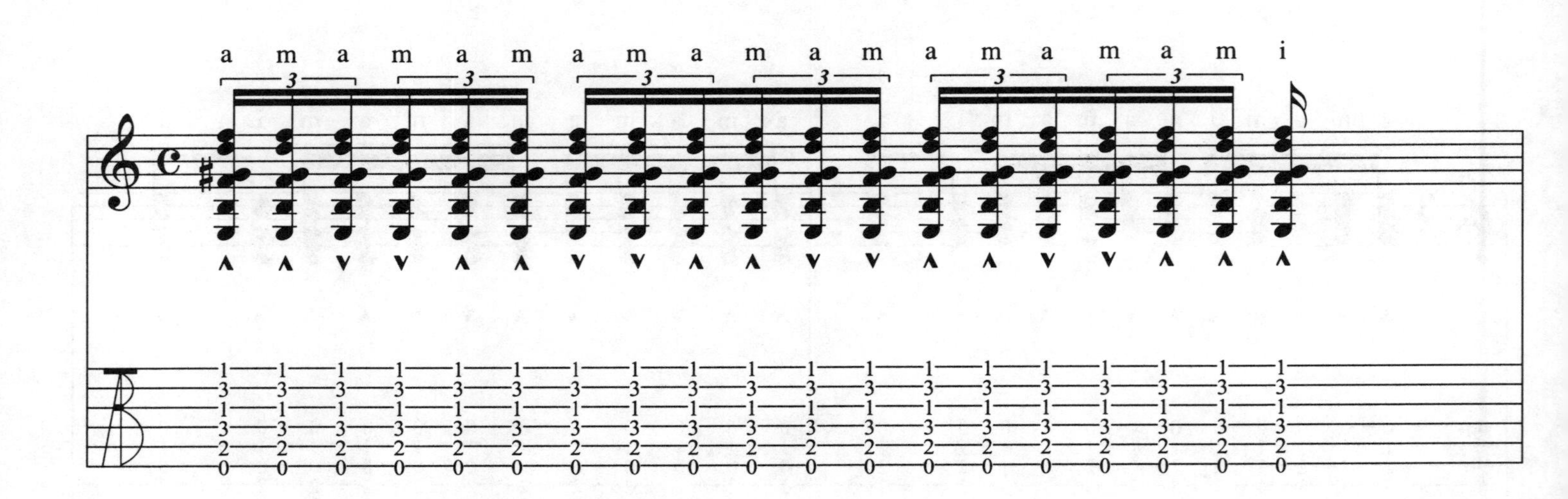

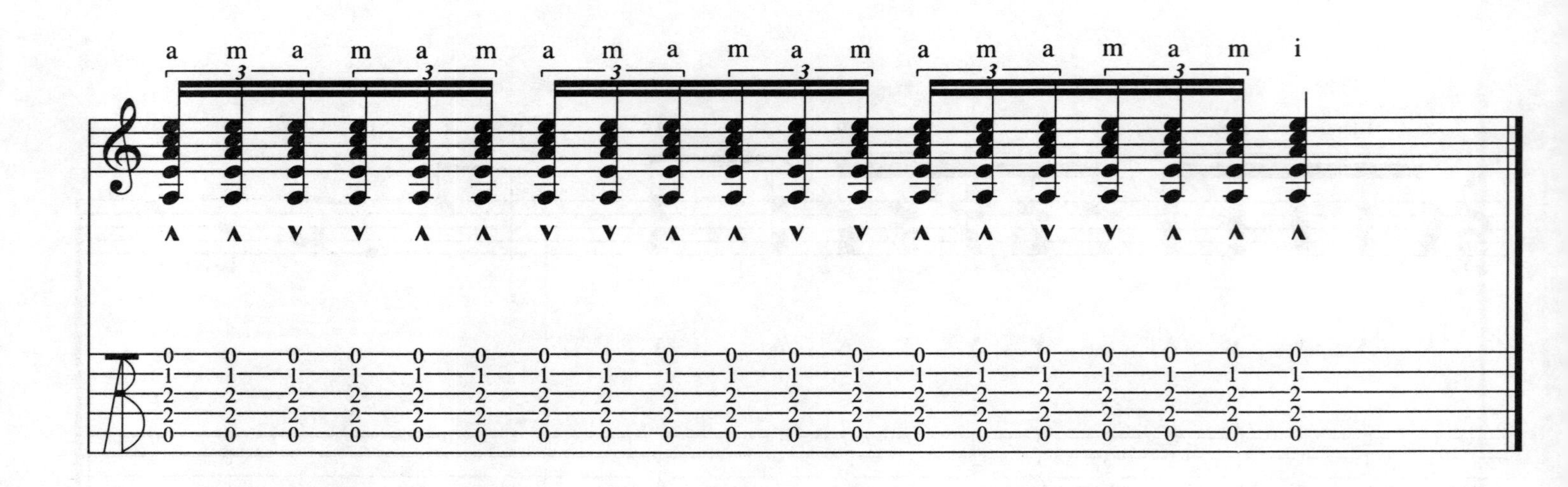

The final example for this pattern is for the execution of a continuous roll without specific rhythmic structure. On this example the rhythmic values are approximations; the example is written in the form of Taranto;

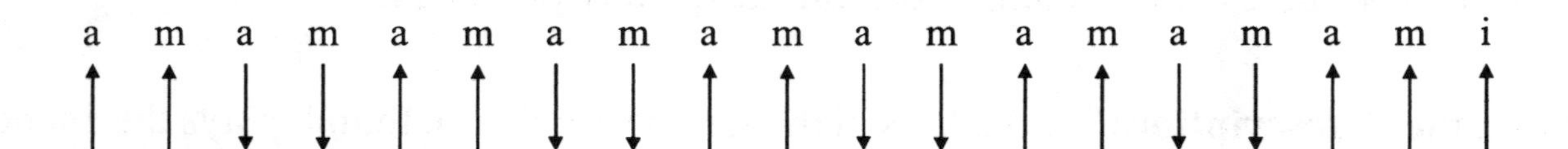

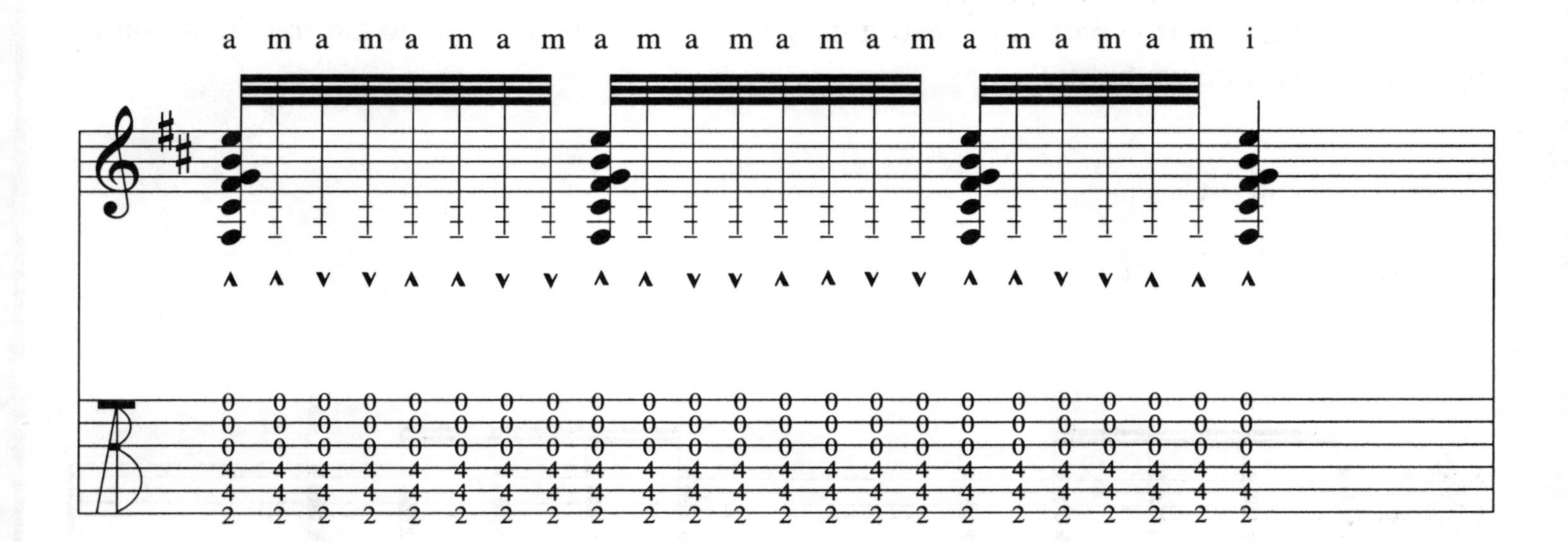

Notice that the pattern ends on the index finger, a finger that is otherwise not used during the execution of the rasgueado.

16th-note rasgueados

The **pami** rasgueado:

This is the same as the Pepe Romero *peami* version, minus the little finger; it produces a steady flow of 16th notes or even 32nd notes, if adequately practiced.

Movement description: The hand is in the free position. The thumb plays the 1st note with an upstroke, the ring finger plays the 2nd with a downstroke, the middle finger plays the 3rd with a downstroke, and the index finger plays the 4th with a downstroke. The wrist stays fairly stationary while the ami part is performed and it only moves slightly upwards to aid the thumb on its upstroke. Therefore we have:

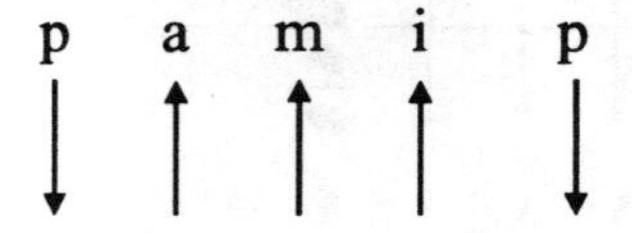

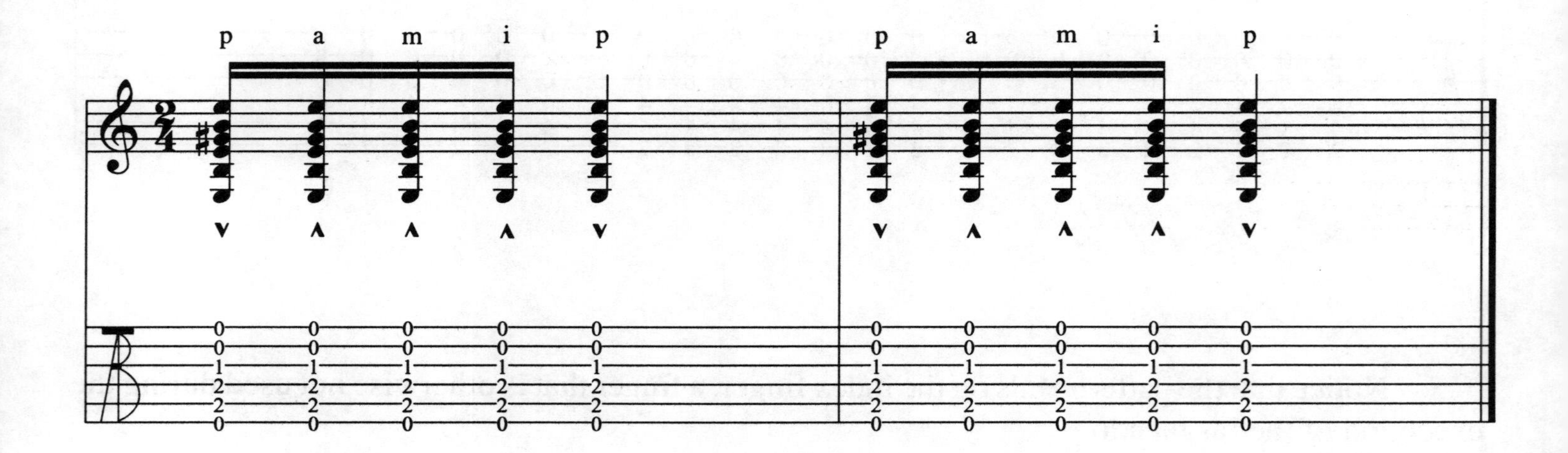

Merengue De Cordoba, the teacher of Manolo Sanlucar, Vincente Amigo and Jose Antonio Rodriguez showed me this specific technique .

The **paip** rasgueado:

Movement description: The hand is in free position. The thumb plays the 1st note with an upstroke, the ring finger plays the 2nd with a downstroke, the index finger plays the 3rd with a downstroke, and the thumb plays the 4th with a downstroke. The wrist stays fairly stationary while the "ai" part is performed and it only moves slightly upwards to aid the thumb on its upstroke and slightly downwards on its downstroke. Therefore we have:

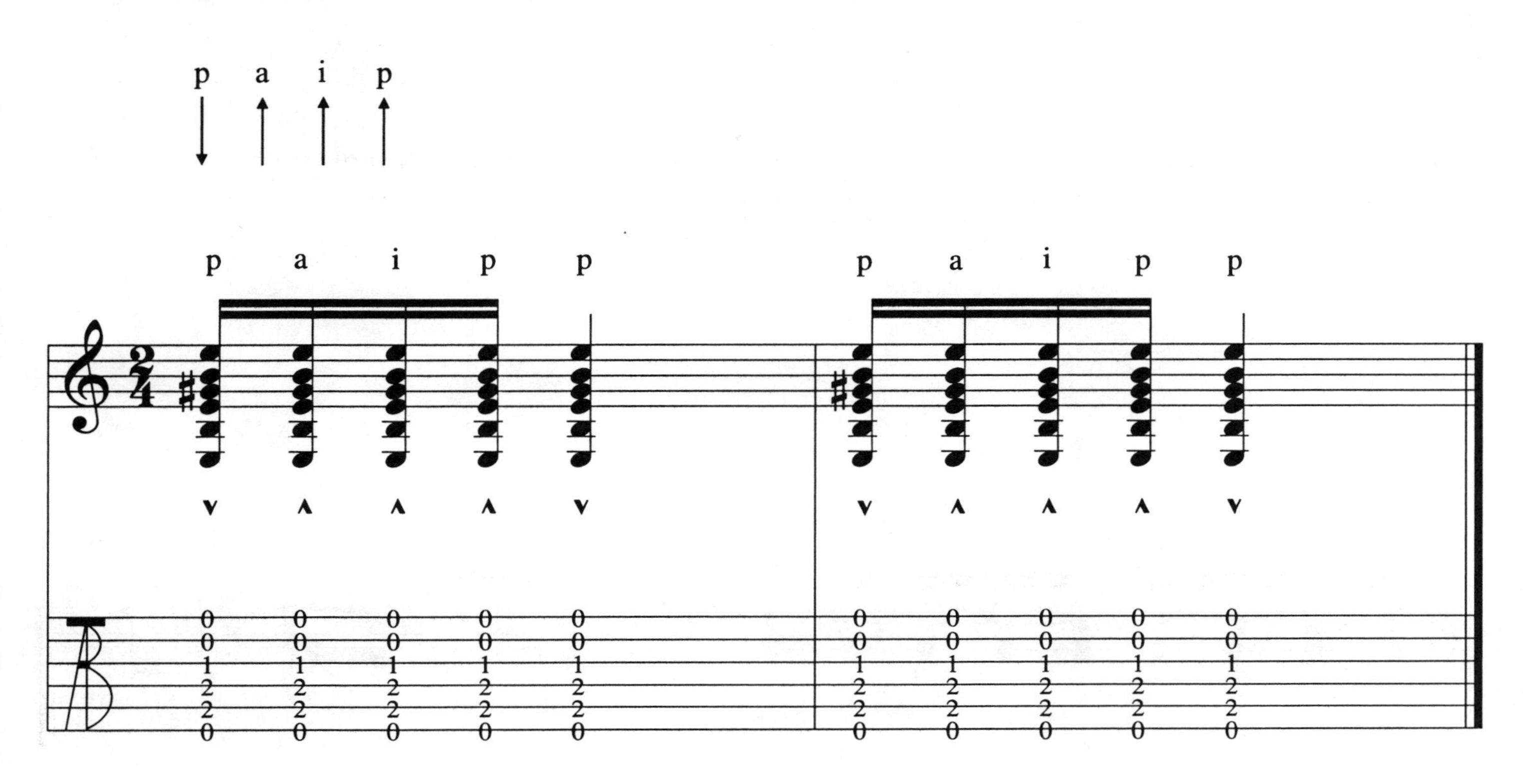

Here's the basic compas of Soleares played using this rasgueado pattern;

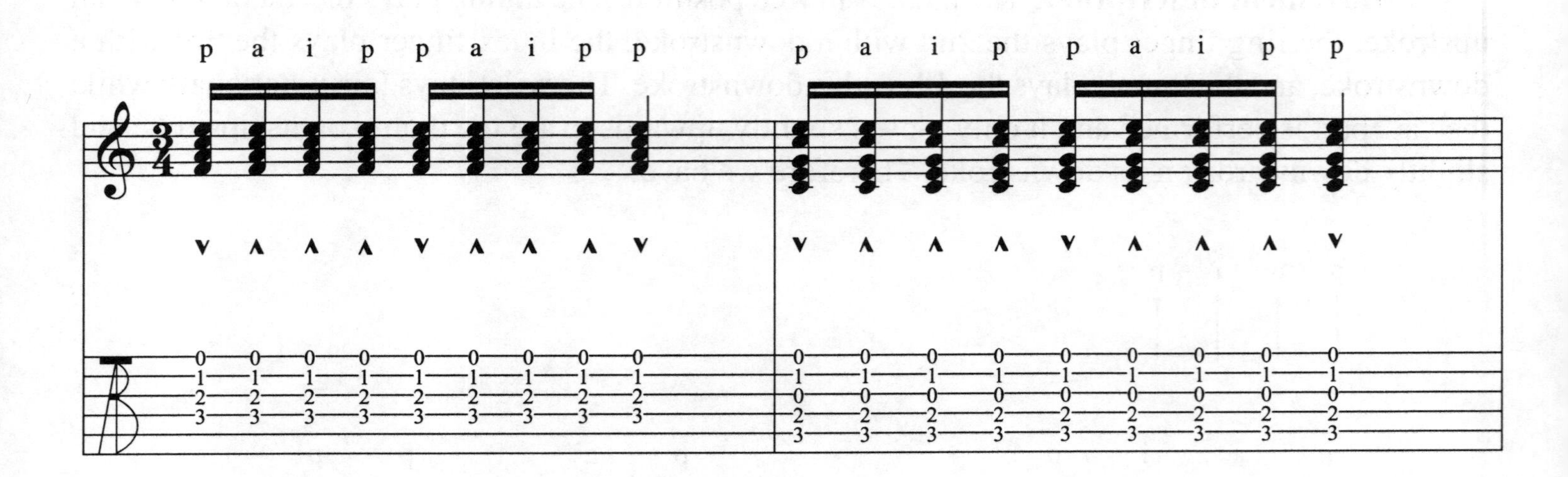

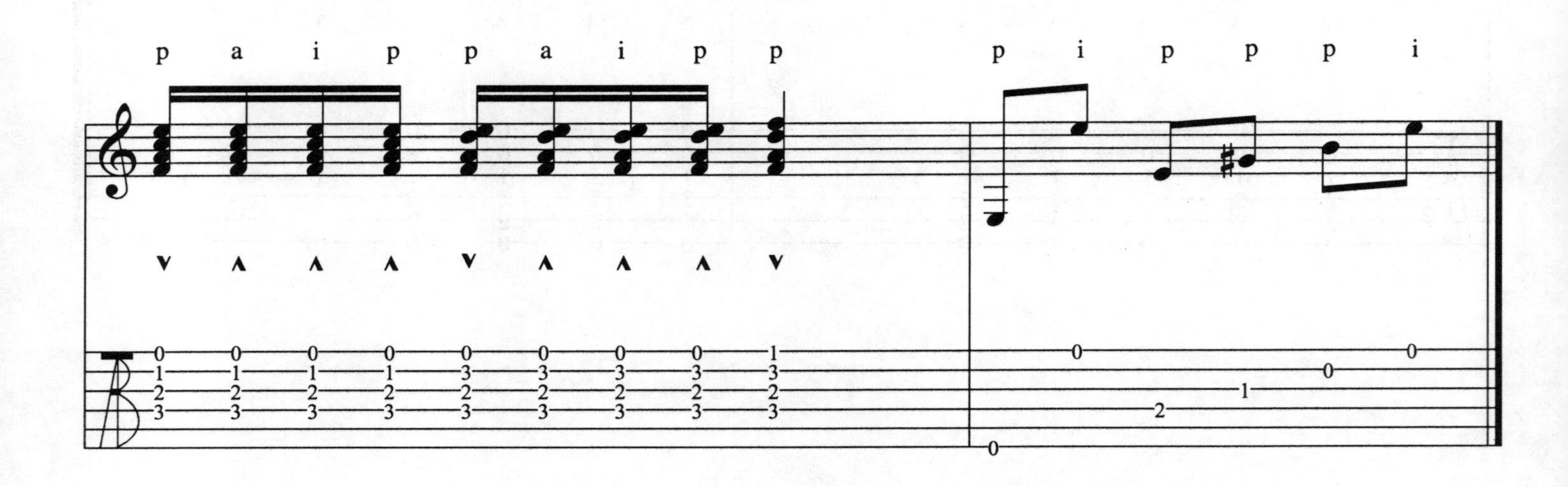

Specific Purpose Rasgueados

Triplet and sextuplet rasgueados

The **pm** rasgueado:

This deceptively simple rasgueado pattern offers a refreshingly different approach to playing triplets. Until now we have examined triplet rasgueados and 16th note rasgueados, as well as quintuplets and triplet rasgueados played in groups of 16th notes. This rasgueado takes a group of 2 strums and plays them in triplet fashion. This is very effective since we have the downbeat alternately being played by an upstroke, then by a downstroke and it gives a very syncopated feel to the rhythm.

Movement description: The hand is in free position. The thumb plays the 1st note with an upstroke, the middle finger plays the 2nd with a downstroke, the thumb plays the 3rd with an upstroke, and the middle plays the 4th with a downstroke.

We will examine this example first in triplets:

p m p m p m p

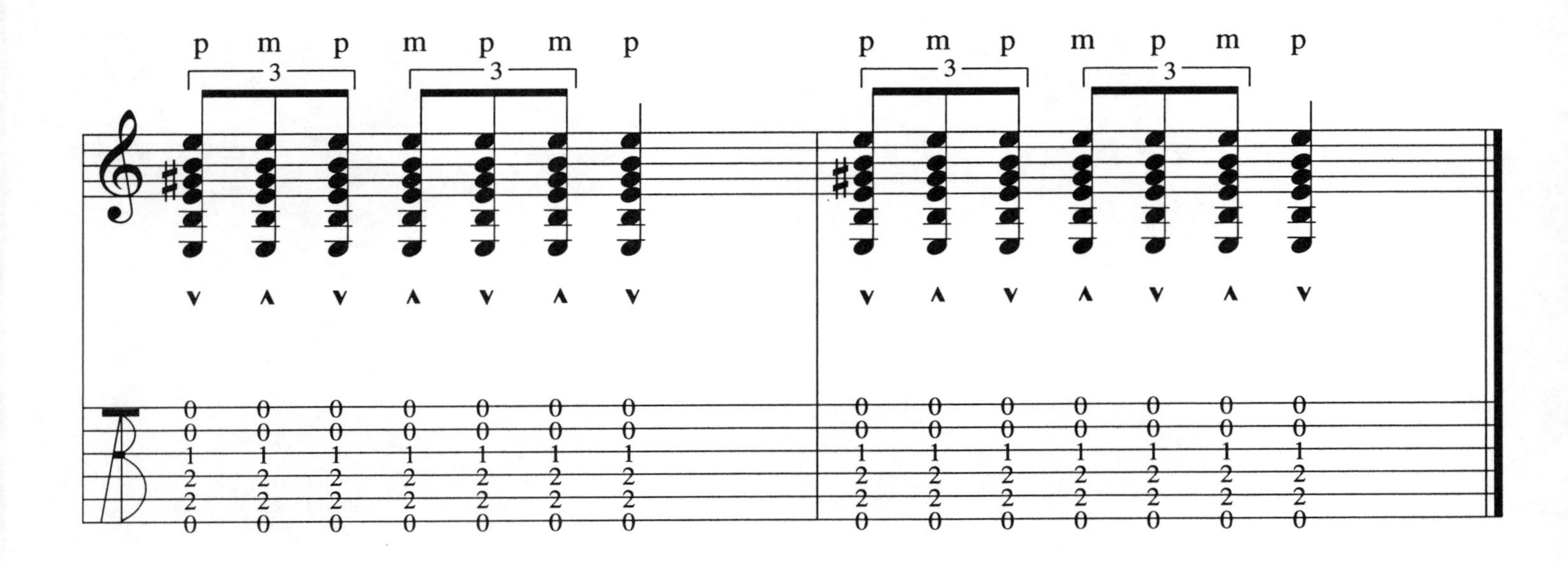

And now, in sextuplets:

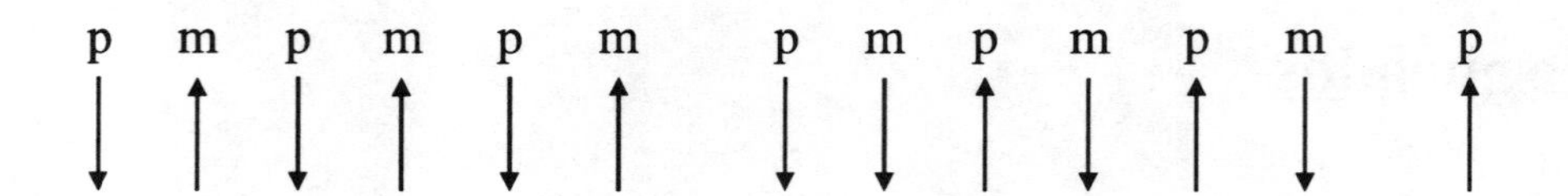

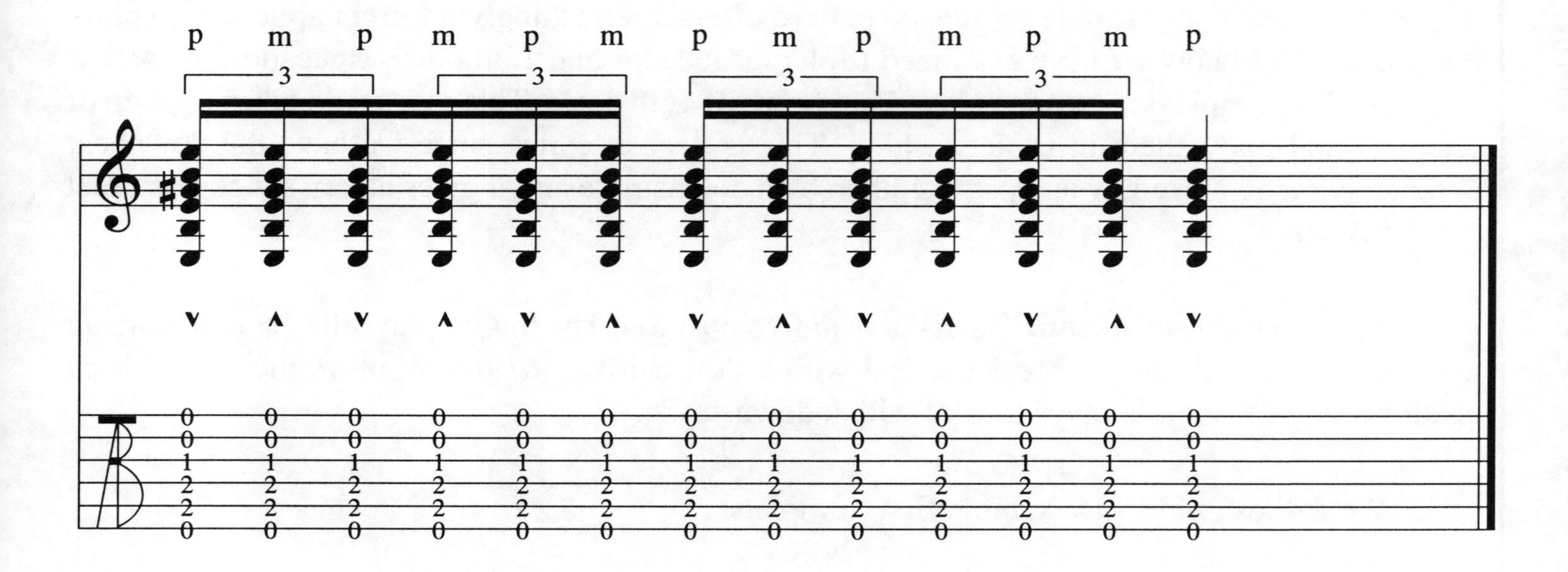

Juan Martin showed this pattern to me; he uses it a lot when accompanying dance, both for its pronounced rhythmic characteristics and for the very loud sound and syncopation it produces.

The **ieam ieam ieam i** rasgueado

This is a sextuplet rasgueado.

Movement description: The hand position is the same as the basic rasgueados. The thumb rests lightly on the 6th string. All other RH fingers are loosely curled in the palm in a very relaxed way. The index finger is flicked out, then the little finger, followed by the ring, the middle and finally, the index finger. Repeat twice. Therefore, we have:

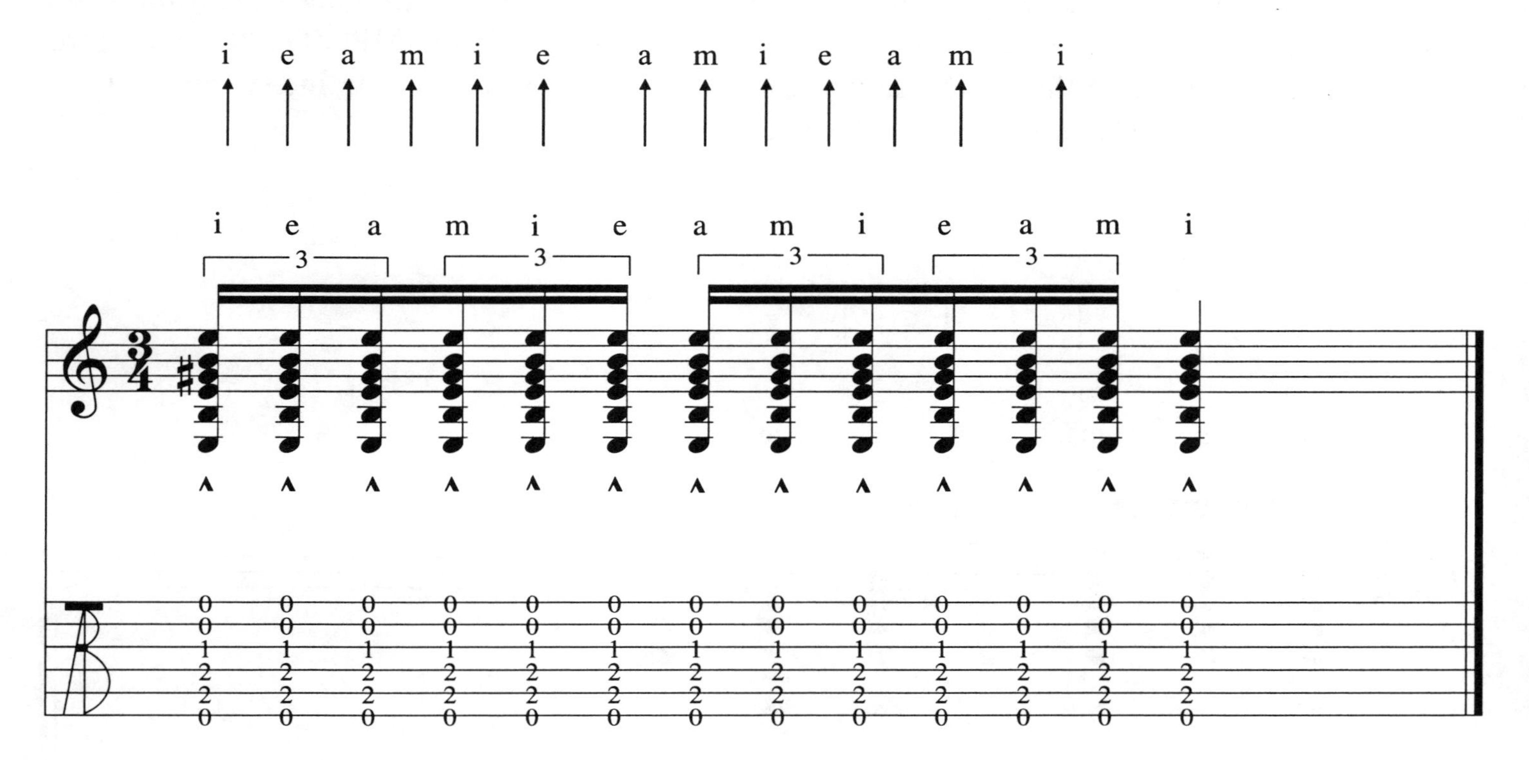

Be very careful with the timing of this pattern, since now we are playing sextuplets and not 16th notes.

The **iam iam i** rasgueado:

This is a pattern that I devised in order to play sextuplets; it is a variation on Juan Serrano's _ieami_ pattern, leaving out the little finger. This makes the pattern very even and easy to use, since it leaves out the finger that is usually the weak link in any rasgueado pattern.

Movement description: The hand position is the same as the basic rasgueado the thumb rests lightly on the 6th string. All other RH fingers are loosely curled in the palm in a very relaxed way. The index finger is flicked out, then the ring finger, followed by the middle, the index, the ring, the middle, and finally, exactly on the beat, the index finger. VERY IMPORTANT: The secret to mastering this move is that at the same time the ring finger strums, the index returns to its original position, poised and ready to strike again.

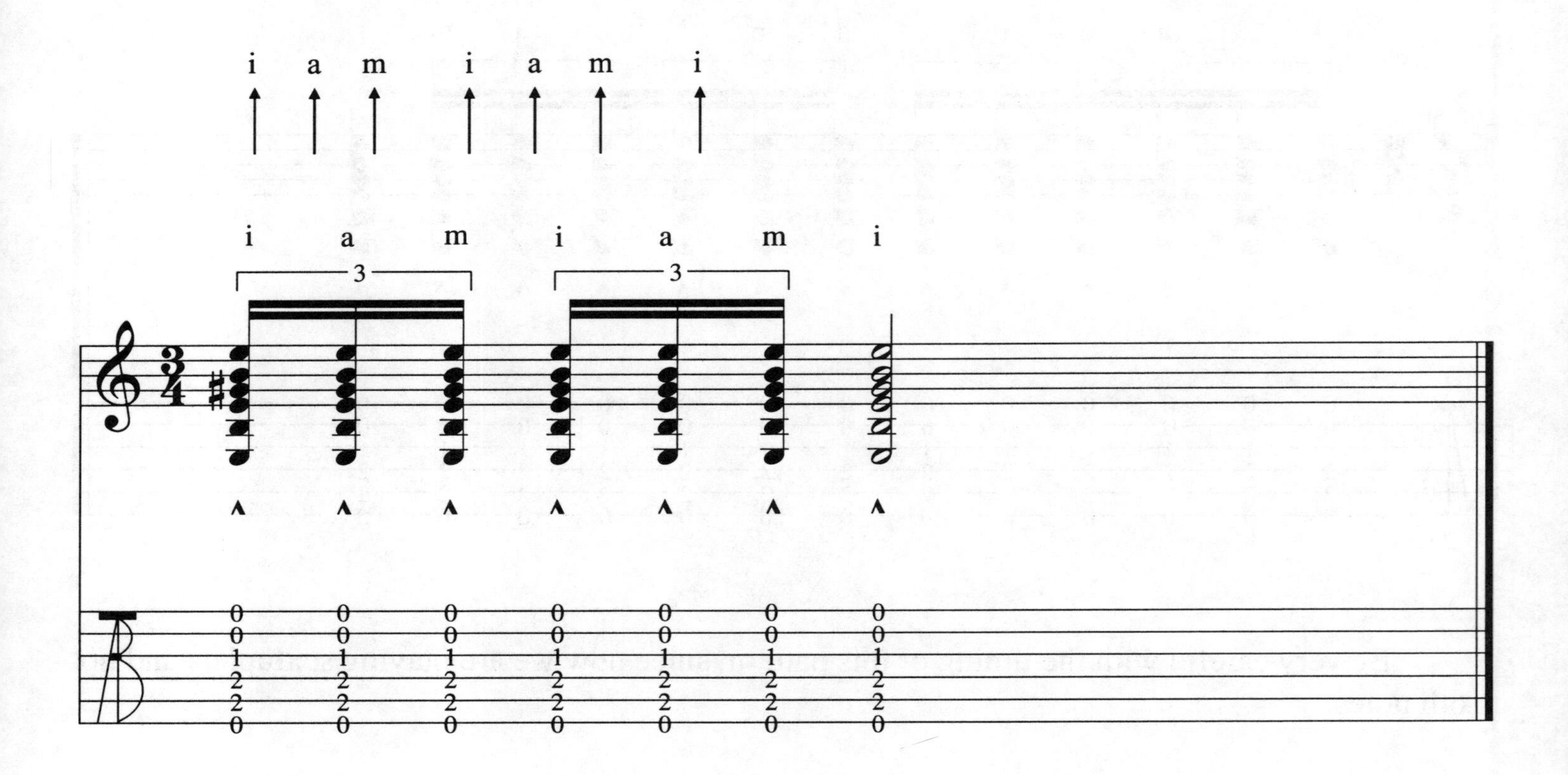

Miscellaneous other rasgueados

The following pattern has two different uses; It can be used as a 2- beat quintuplet pattern if played twice or as a 16th note 3-beat pattern if played 3 times.

The **ami** rasgueado:

This is a short, 3-note rasgueado, which is often used as an ornament in place of the *eami*, especially in Bulerias, where the tempo is too fast to comfortably fit a 4-note rasgueado as an ornament.

Movement description: The hand position is the same as the basic rasgueado. The thumb rests lightly on the 6th string. All other RH fingers are loosely curled in the palm in a very relaxed way. The ring finger is flicked out, then the middle finger, followed by the index finger. The index finger strikes exactly on the downbeat of the coming beat.

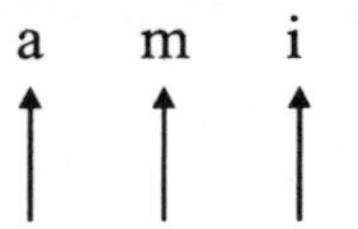

Here's an example, based on the form of Solea por Bulerias.

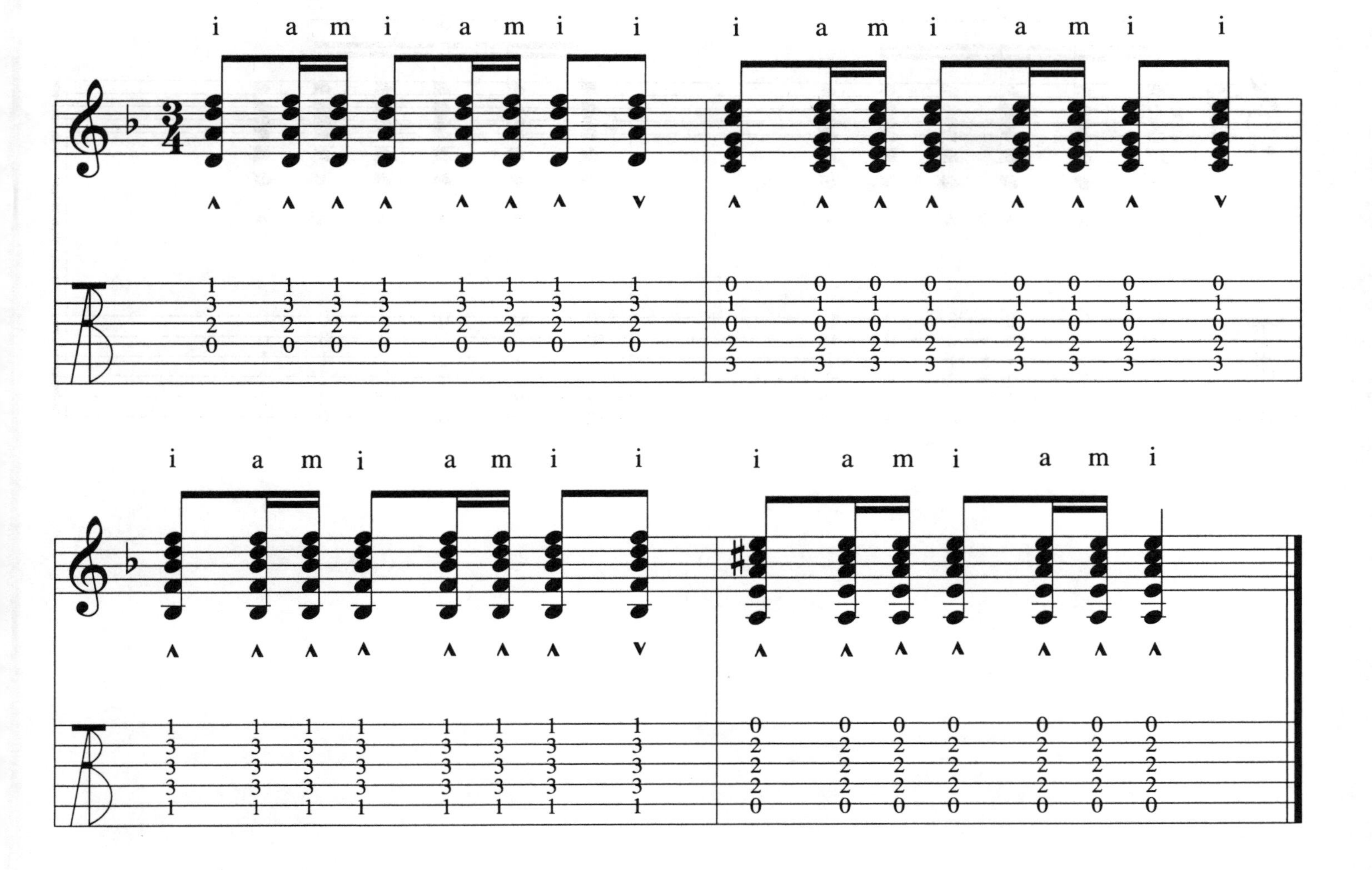

The **amiami** rasgueado:

This rasgueado creates a set of quintuplets, very useful for medium tempo forms, when 16th notes are too slow and sextuplets are too fast.

Movement description: The hand position is the same as the basic rasgueado. The thumb rests lightly on the 6th string. All other RH fingers are loosely curled in the palm in a very relaxed way. The ring finger is flicked out, then the middle finger, followed by the index finger and the movement repeats once more. VERY IMPORTANT: The secret to mastering the flow of this move is that at the same time the index finger strums, the ring finger returns to its original position, poised and ready to strike again.

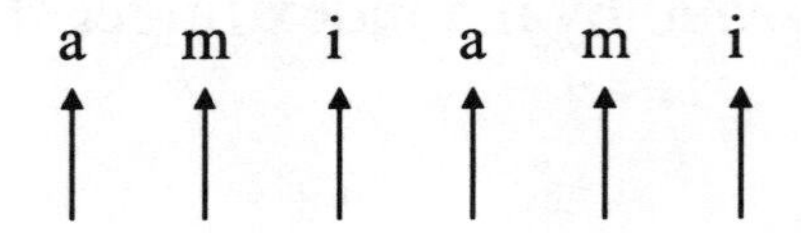

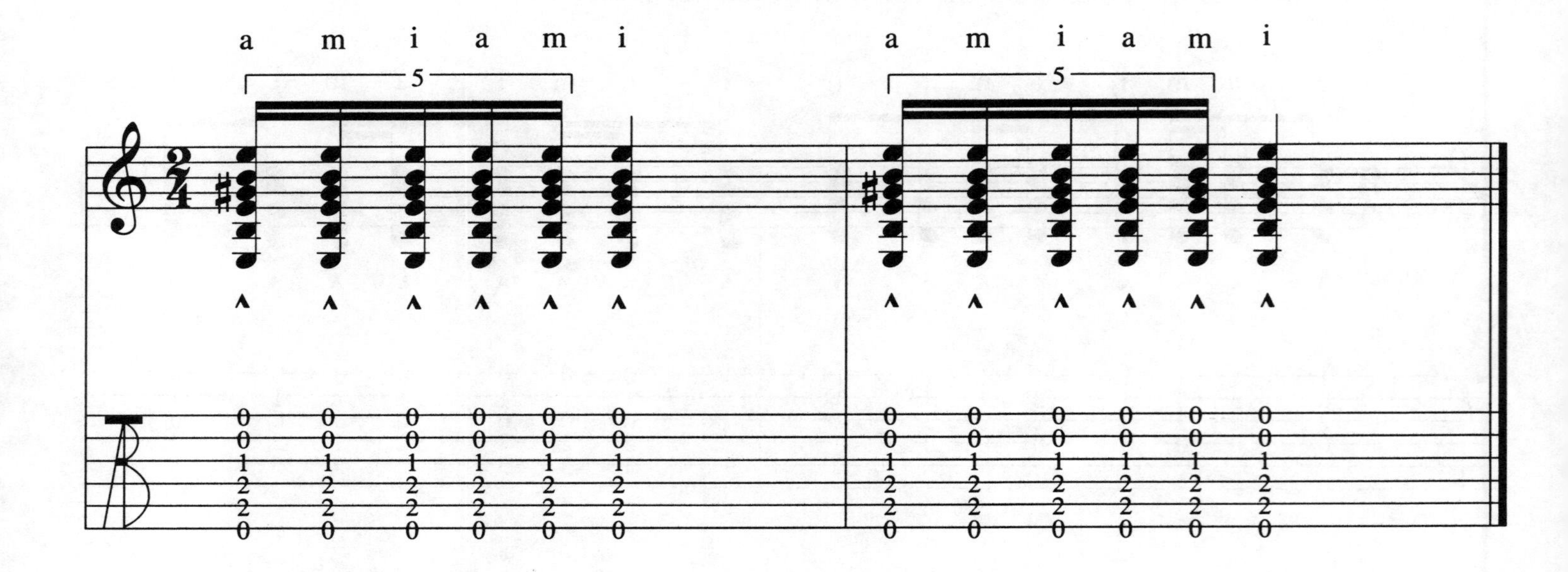

Here's another example; this time based on the form of the Farucca:

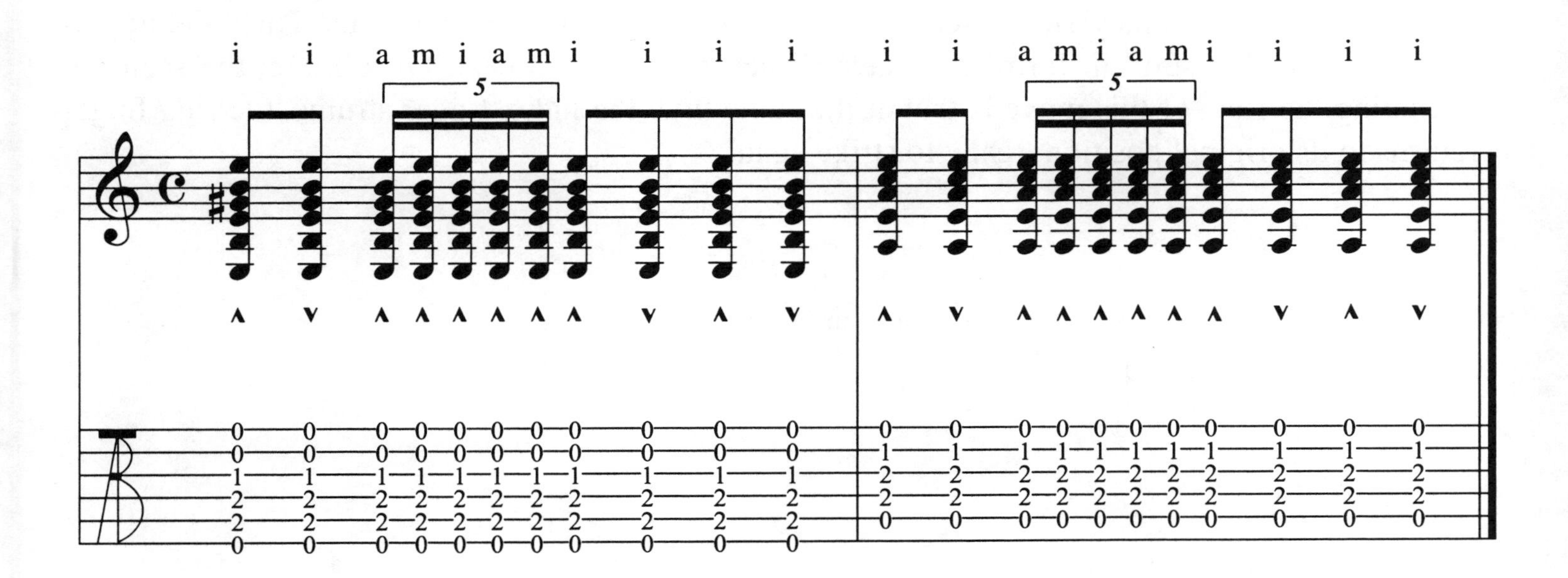

The amiamiami rasgueado:

This second permutation is exactly the same as the previous version with the ami pattern repeated once more; this yields a steady stream of 16th notes spanning 3-beats. This kind of pattern is extremely useful in forms that have an accent every 3rd beat. Once more, the secret to mastering the flow of this move is that at the same time the index finger strums, the ring finger returns to its original position, ready to strike again.

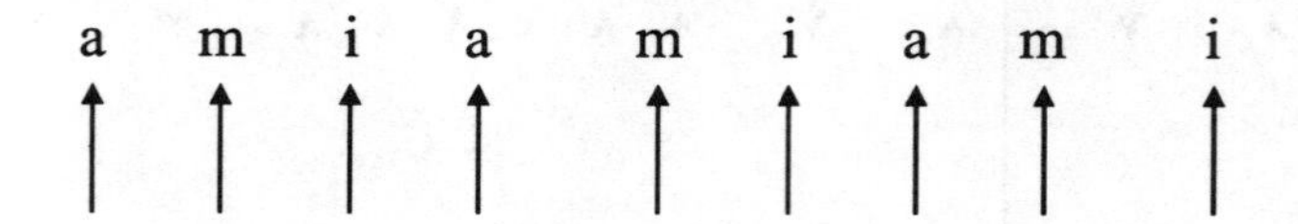

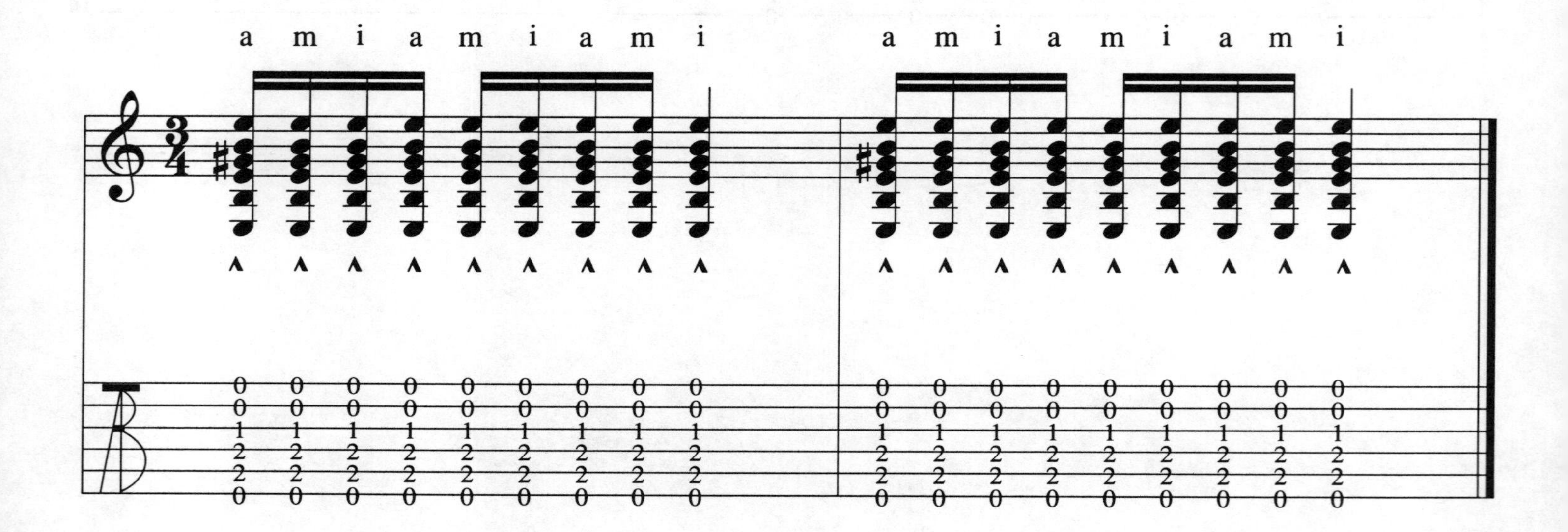

And here's another example in Alegrias in E:

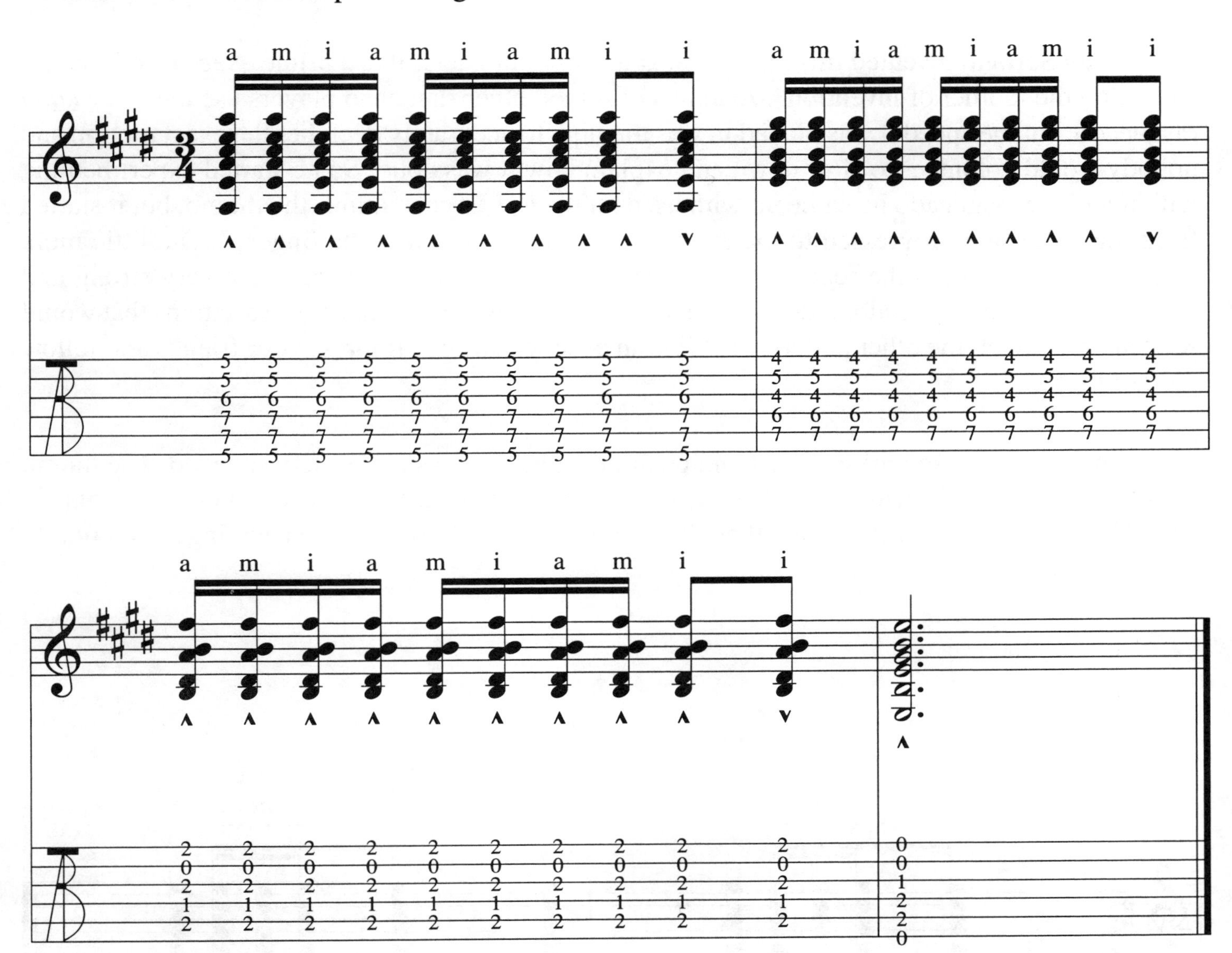

The **imae** rasgueado:

Juan Serrano invented this rasgueado at a very young age. It is a prime example of "necessity being the mother of invention". Juan had observed other flamenco players use the basic <u>*eami*</u> rasgueado, but the speed it was played in was too high to accurately decipher the exact motion and nobody would volunteer to slow down and explain how it was done! So he started experimenting with it and the rasgueado he came up with used all the RH fingers, minus the thumb, but it started from the index and progressed to the middle, ring and finally the little finger! It is a little more difficult to master than the regular <u>*eami*</u> pattern, but in Serrano's hands, it is a very strong and rhythmically even rasgueado. It does not really offer any rhythmic nuances or variations that would set it apart from all the other patterns, but it is an excellent way to impress your friends and fellow guitar players!

Movement description: The hand position is the same as the basic rasgueado. The thumb rests lightly on the 6th string. All other RH fingers are loosely curled in the palm in a very relaxed way. The index finger is flicked out, then the middle finger, followed by the ring finger, and finally the little finger.

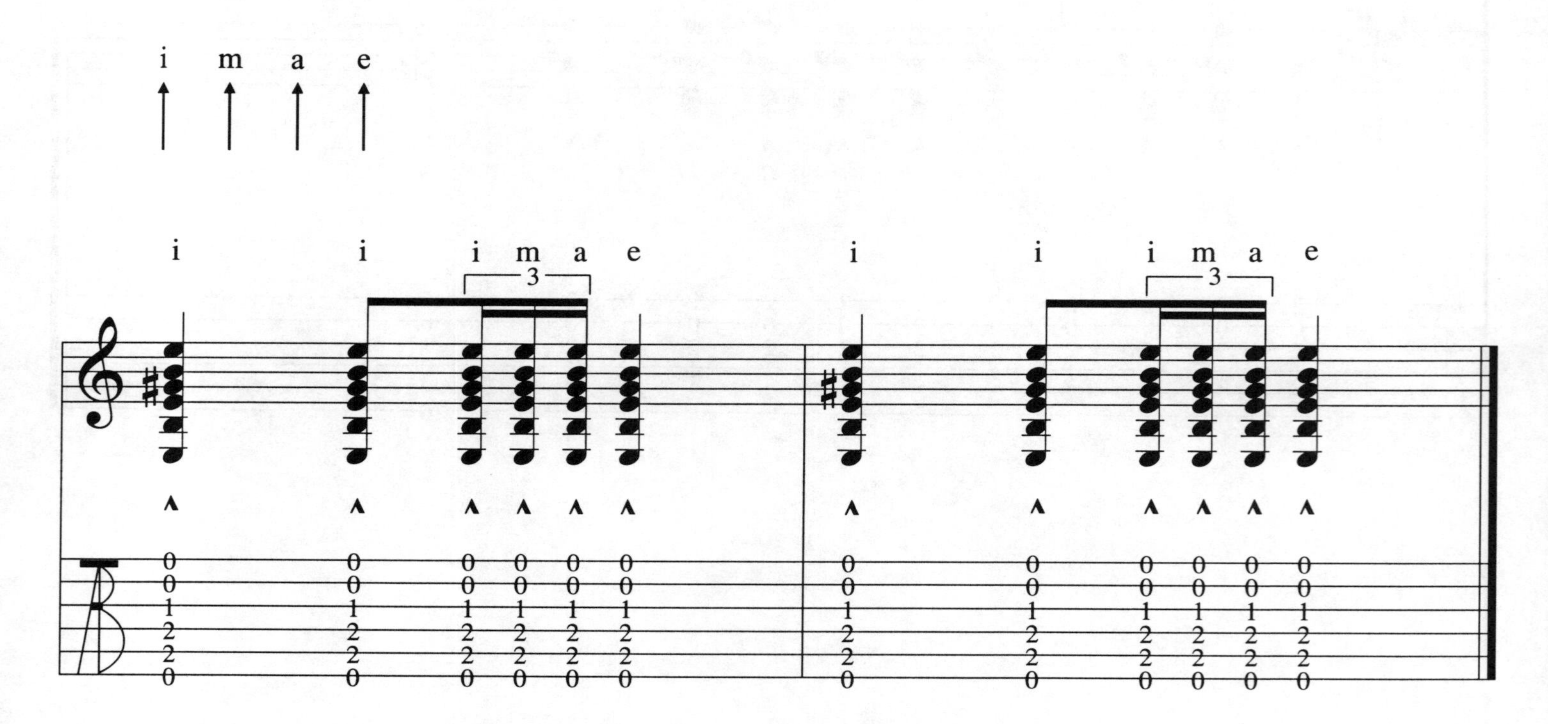

Juan Serrano uses this pattern almost always when he plays Verdiales. Here's an example of Verdiales in E that uses this pattern:

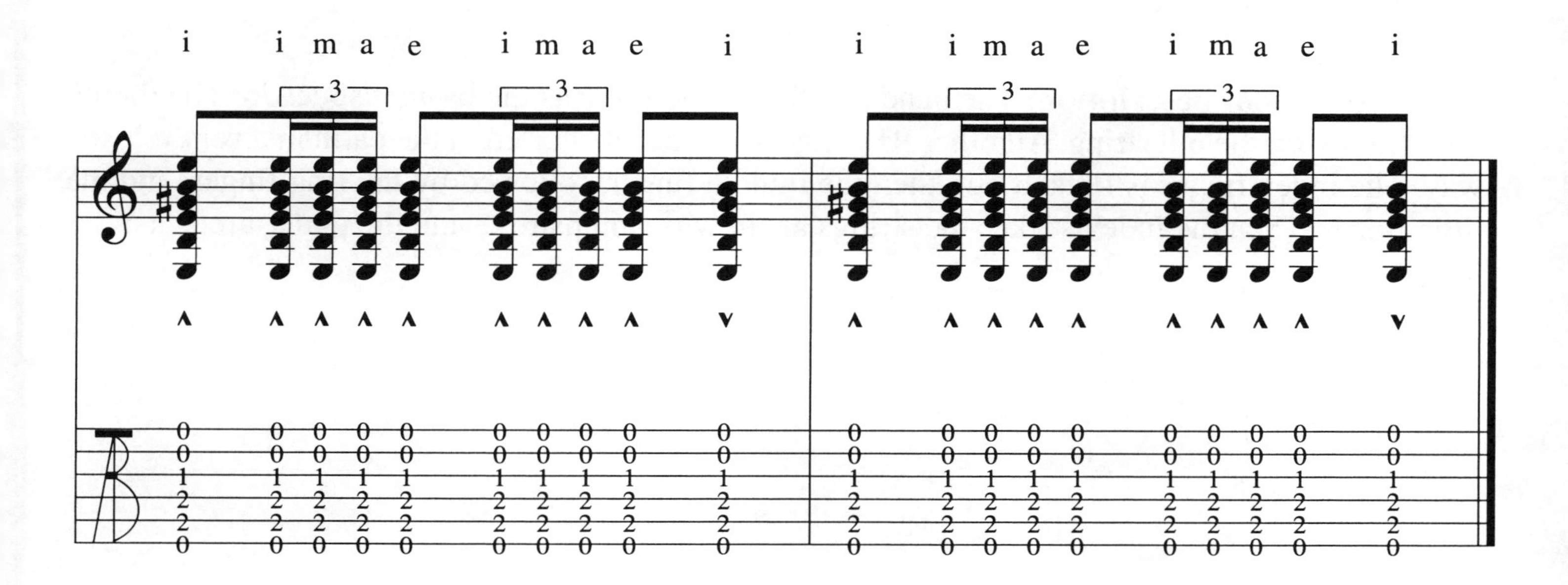

The imaei rasgueado:

In order to create a continuous sound with the imae rasgueado, Serrano resets the pattern with an index upstroke.

Movement description: The hand position is the same as the basic rasgueado. The thumb rests lightly on the 6th string. All other RH fingers are loosely curled in the palm in a very relaxed way. The index finger is flicked out, then the middle finger, followed by the ring finger, and the little finger. Then the index strikes the strings again with an upstroke and the pattern repeats:

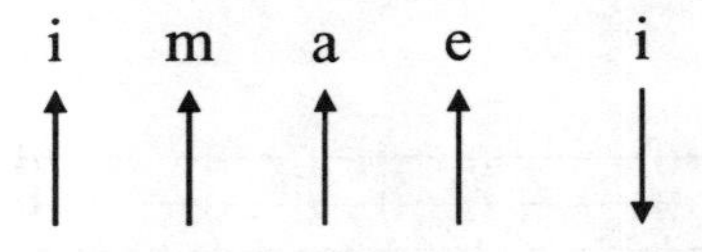

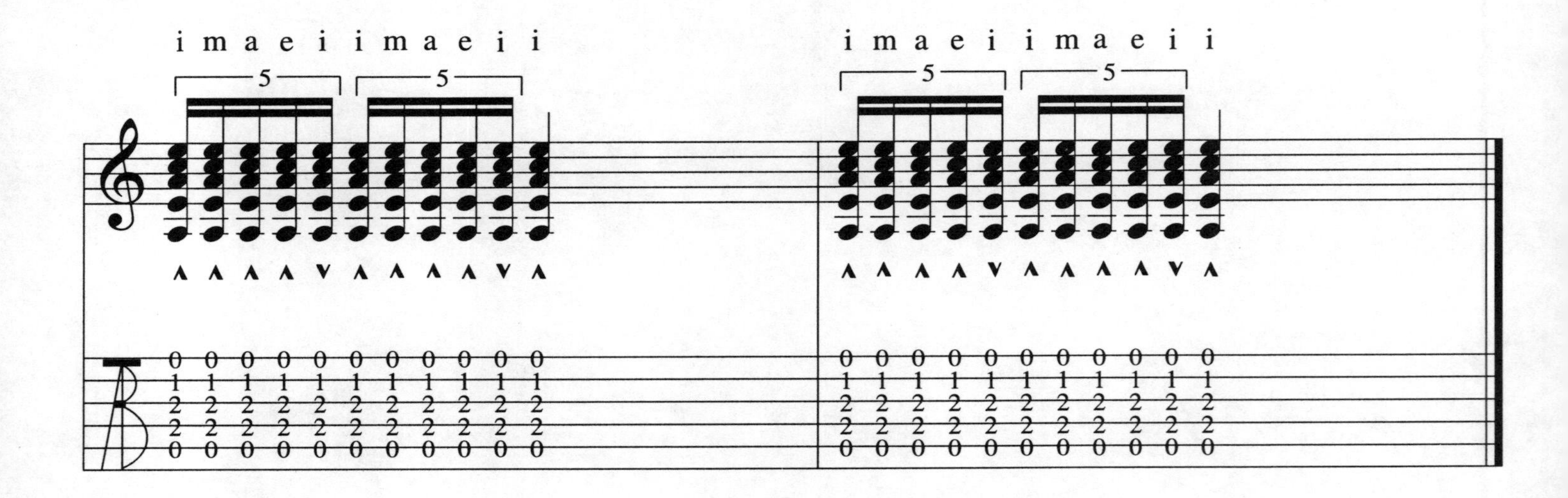

When repeated, this pattern has the same phrasing as Sabicas' *eamii* pattern; it is played in quintuplets. Here's another example; the basic Soleares rhythm played with this rasgueado.

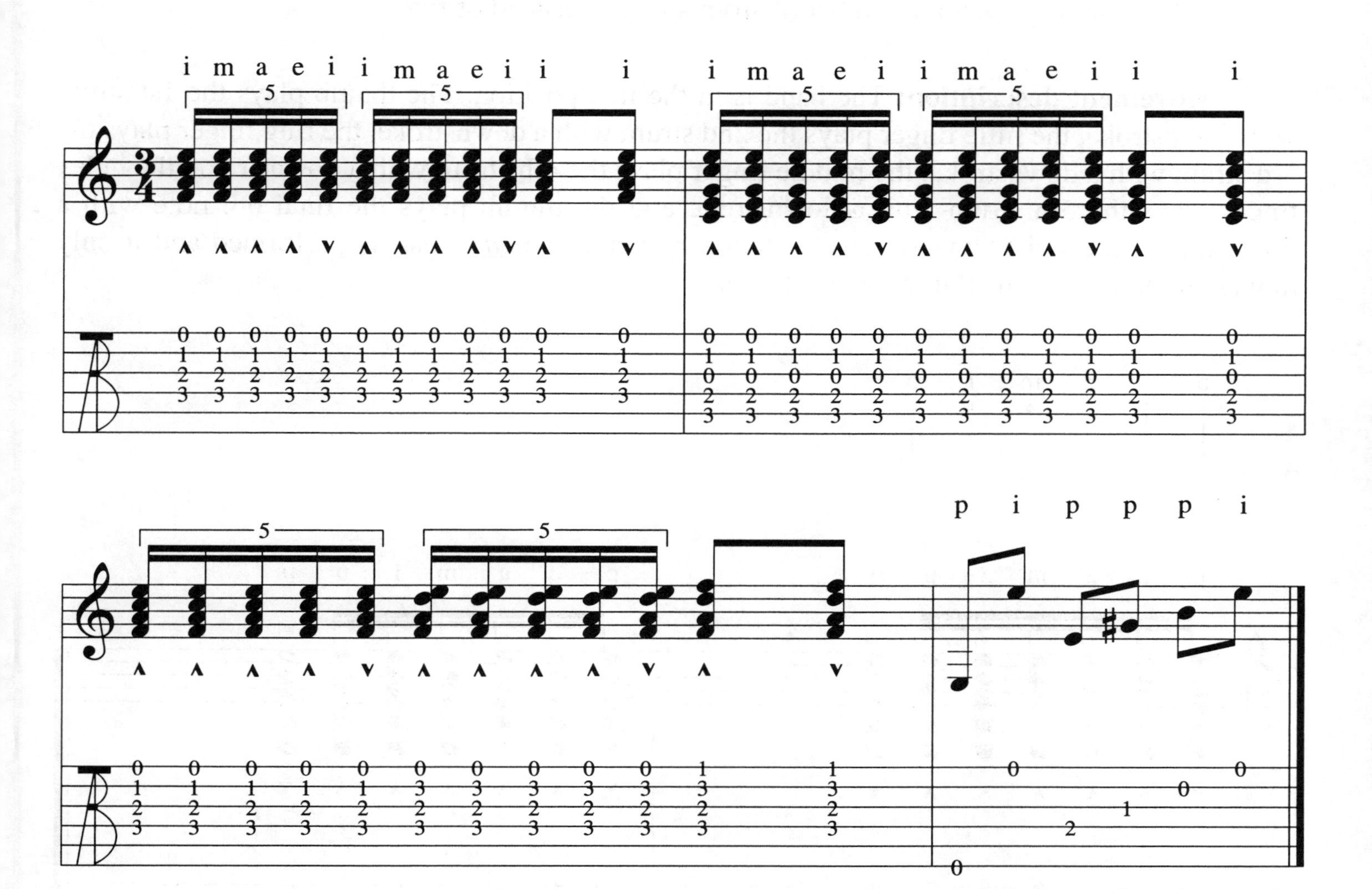

The **peamip** rasgueado

This is a very interesting sextuplet pattern, since it uses all the fingers of the right hand, including both an upstroke and a downstroke from the thumb! It is based on the Pepe Romero *peami* quintuplet pattern. However, in this form a thumb downstroke is added after the index downstroke, bringing the total number of strums to six, instead of five.

Movement description: The hand is in the free position. The thumb plays the 1st strum with an upstroke, the little finger plays the 2nd strum with a downstroke, the ring finger plays the 3rd strum with a downstroke, the middle finger plays the 4th strum with a downstroke, the index finger plays the 5th strum with a downstroke and the thumb plays the final 6th note with a downstroke. The wrist stays relatively stationary while the *eami* part is performed and it only moves slightly to aid the thumb on its strums.

Here's an example where this pattern is used to end a musical phrase with a quick sextuplet, with a duration of 2 beats. This example is based on the form of the Farucca.

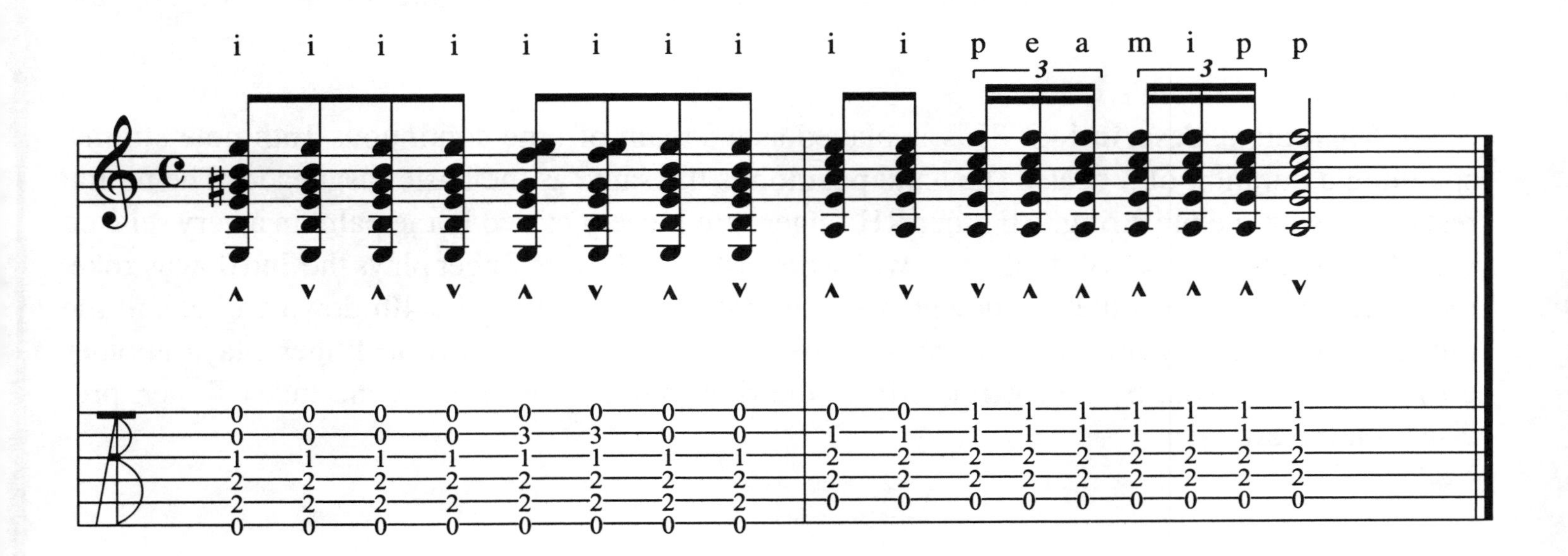

The **eami ieam i** rasgueado:

This is a combination of the 5-note *eamii* rasgueado, plus the basic rasgueado pattern *eami*. This is a very handy pattern for forms that have accents every 3 beats, like Soleares, Alegrias and Bulerias.

Movement description: This is played as a stream of nine continuous 16th note strums, spanning a duration of 3 beats. The hand position is the same as the basic rasgueado. The thumb rests lightly on the 6th string. All other RH fingers are loosely curled in the palm in a very relaxed way. The little finger plays the 1st strum with a downstroke, the ring finger plays the 2nd downstroke, the middle finger plays the 3rd downstroke, the index finger plays the 4th downstroke, and the index finger plays again, but with an upstroke this time. Then the little finger plays another downstroke, followed by downstrokes from the ring, middle and, finally, the index finger, precisely on the 3rd beat.

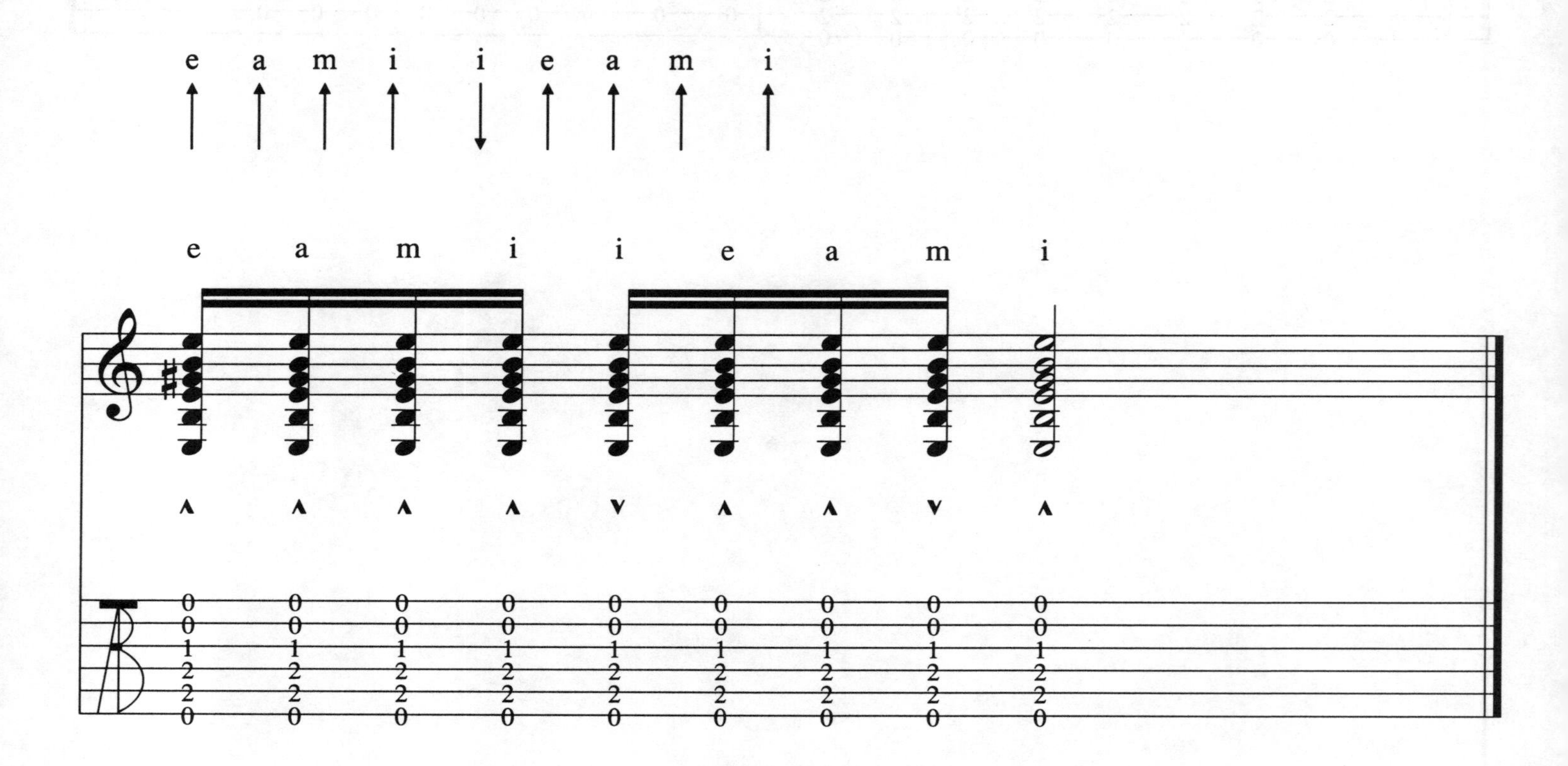

Here's an example of this pattern, in the style of Soleares:

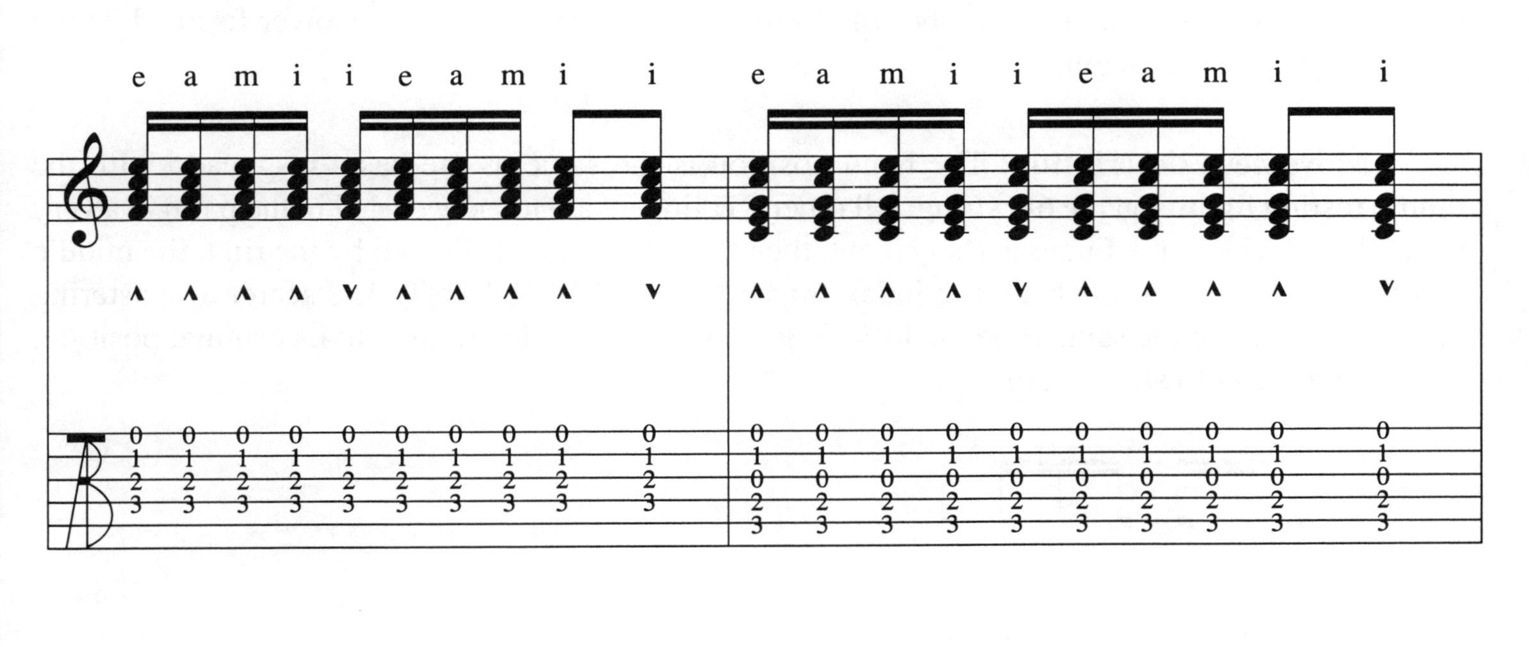

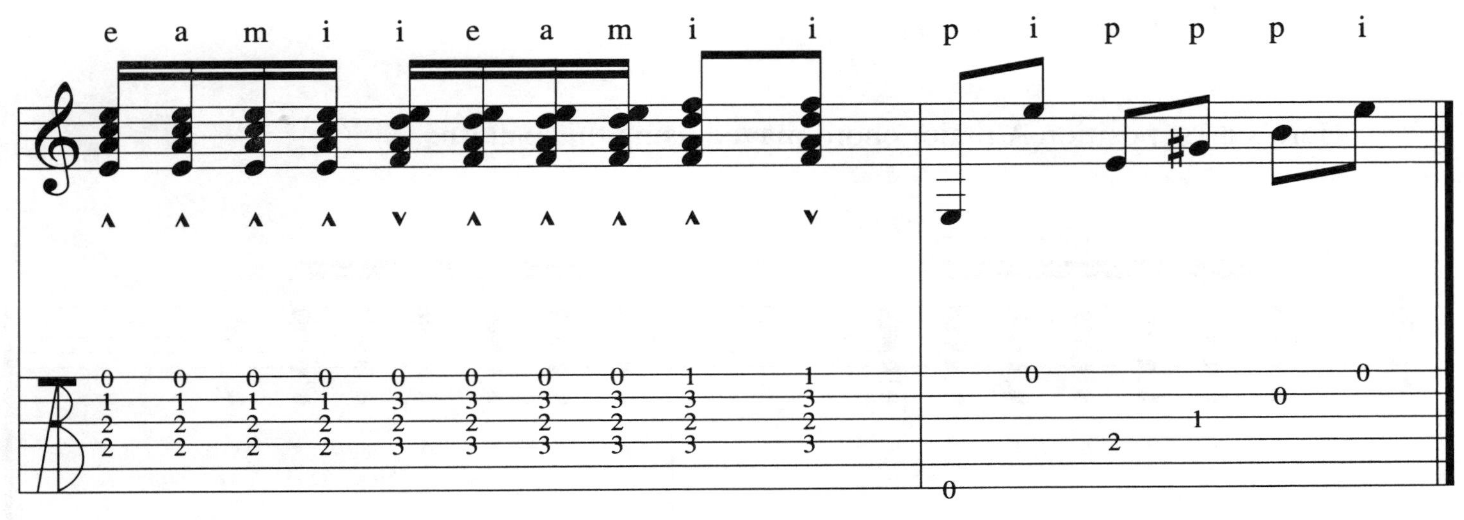

The **ieamii** rasgueado:

This is a combination of the Juan Serrano 5-note ieami rasgueado, with an added index upstroke. This brings the total number of strums up to 6. Very useful for slower forms, like the Farucca, Tientos and Seguiriyas.

Movement description: The hand position is the same as the basic rasgueado with the thumb resting lightly on the 6th string. All other RH fingers are loosely curled in the palm in a very relaxed way. The index finger is flicked out, then the little finger, followed by the ring, the middle and finally, exactly on the beat, the index finger. VERY IMPORTANT: The secret to mastering this move is that at the same time the little finger strums, the index returns to its original position, poised and ready to strike again.

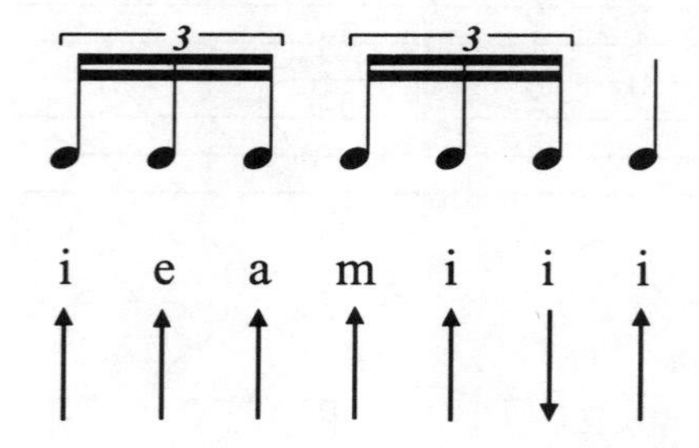

Here's a 1st position A major chord played using this pattern:

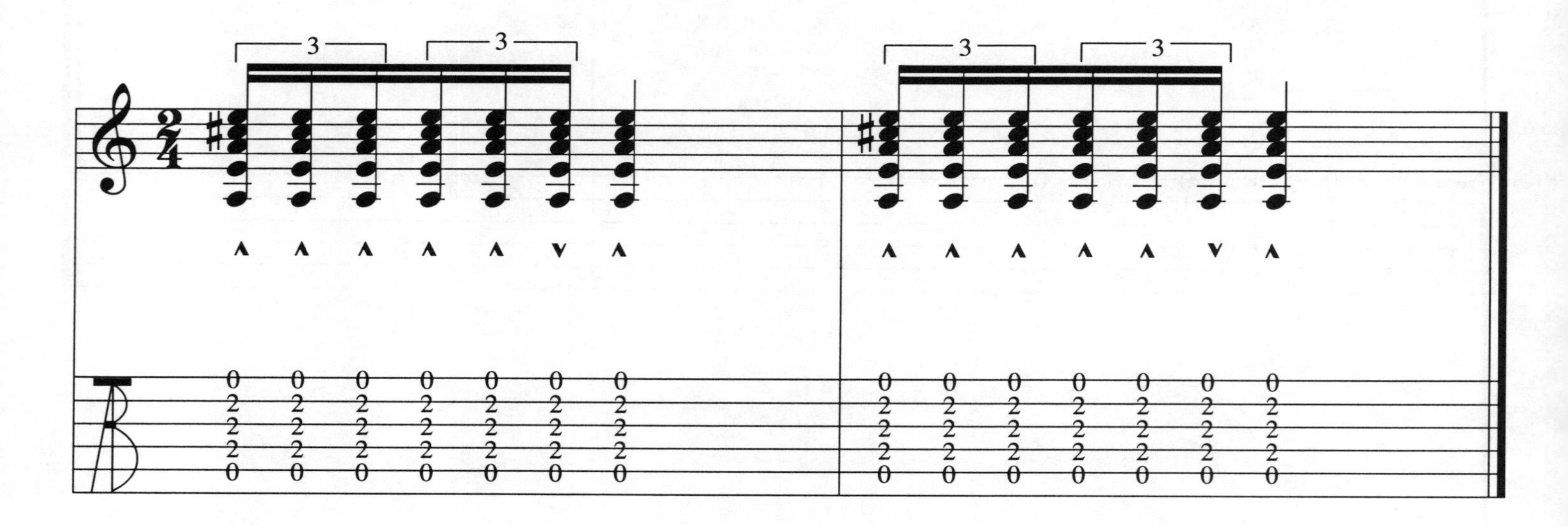

The **amiamiami** Rasgueado

The following pattern is very useful for continuous rolls; however, it is not very rhythmically pronounced. This is a very helpful pattern for forms that have accent every 3 beats, like Soleares, Alegrias and Bulerias.

Movement description: The hand stays in the basic position. First the ring finger plays a downstroke, the middle finger plays a downstroke, the index finger plays a downstroke, the ring finger plays an upstroke, the middle finger plays a upstroke, the index finger plays an upstroke, the ring finger plays a downstroke, the middle finger plays a downstroke and finally the index finger plays a downstroke exactly on the beat. It looks on paper much harder than it really is, just follow the pattern slowly and you will very easily be able to see the logic behind it.

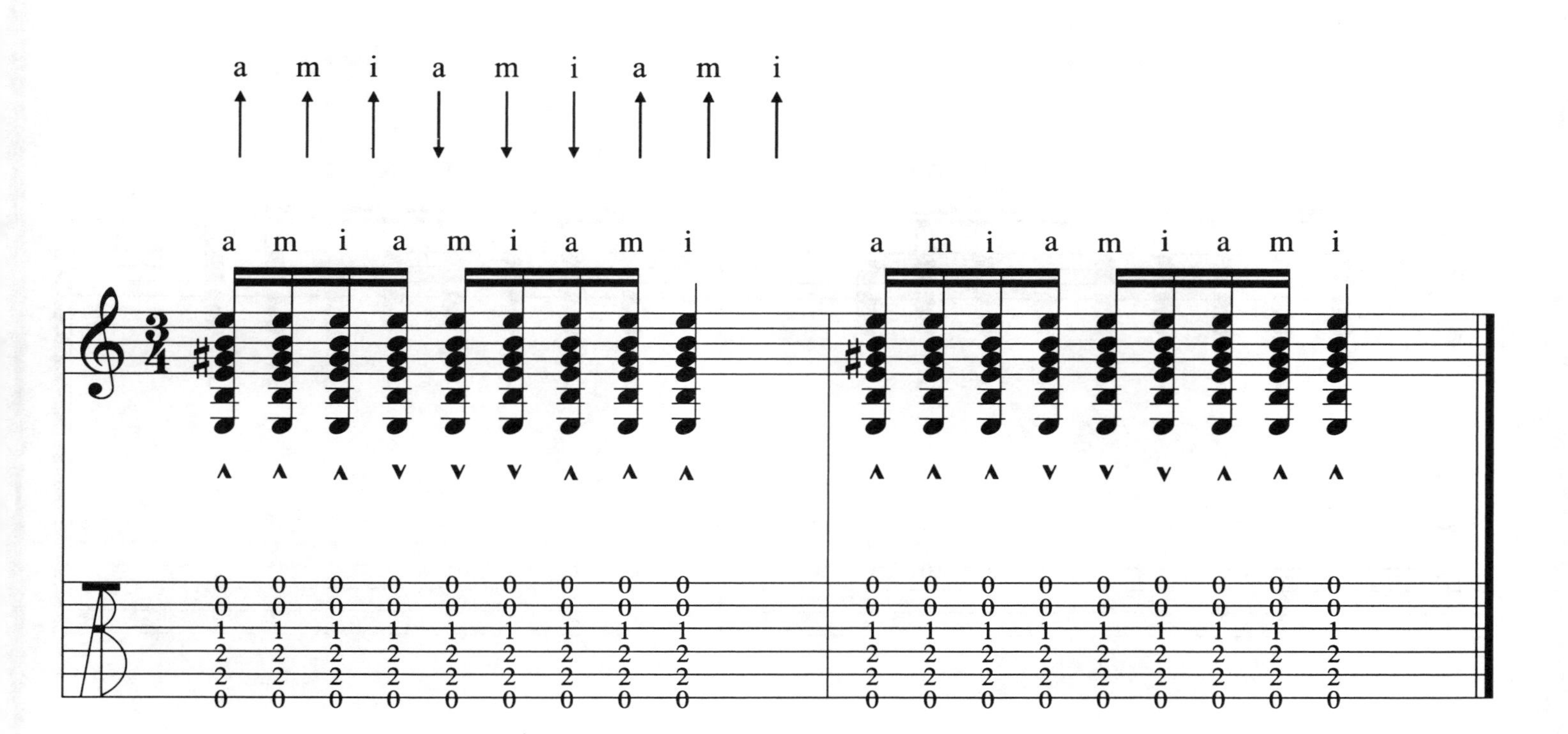

The **amiimami** rasgueado:

This is a pattern I learned from the great classical guitarist and prolific educator, Ricardo Iznaola. Once again, this is a 16th note pattern, with a duration 3-beats.

Movement description: The hand stays in the basic position. First the ring finger plays a downstroke, the middle finger plays a downstroke, the index finger plays a downstroke, the index finger plays an upstroke, the middle finger plays a upstroke, the ring finger plays an upstroke, the ring finger plays a downstroke, the middle finger plays a downstroke and finally the index finger plays a downstroke exactly on the beat. Once again, just follow the pattern slowly and you will very easily be able to see the logic behind it.

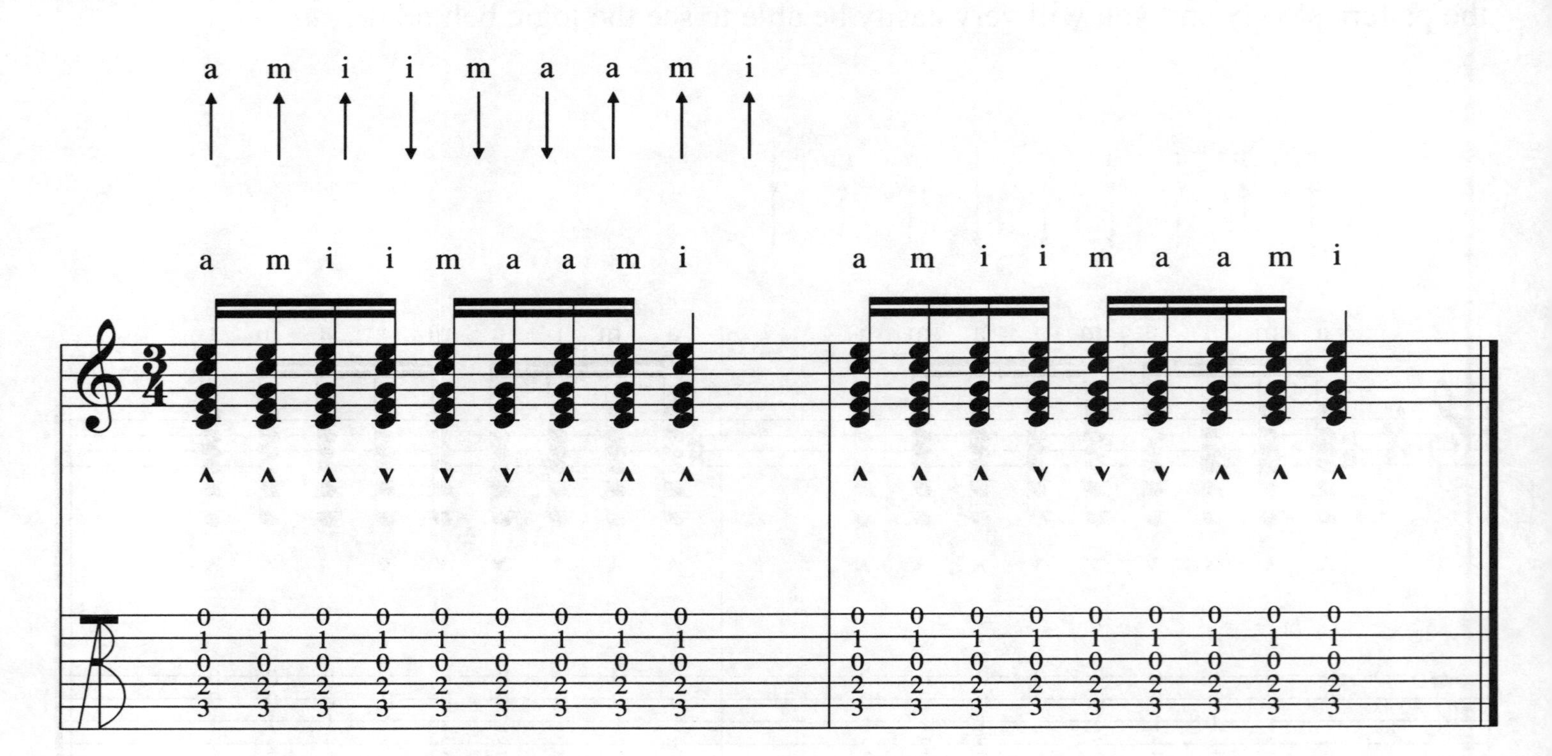

A final rasgueado exercise

Here's a great way to warm up your fingers; this is a noteworthy technique builder as far as rasgueados are concerned.

The hand position is the same as the basic rasgueado. The thumb rests lightly on the 6th string. All other RH fingers are loosely curled in the palm in a very relaxed way. Here is the pattern:

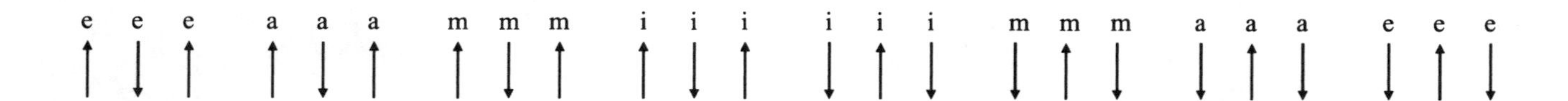

Repeat continuously. Do this VERY slowly and evenly. Play the notes as triplets and later as 16th notes. The purpose of this exercise is to become equally adept at doing upstrokes and downstrokes with all the right hand fingers, apart from the thumb. This way, all your fingers get a good workout. This pattern has very limited practical use but it is a great training tool!

Later you can also add the thumb in this pattern. In this case, the hand will start on the free position and the complete pattern will be as follows:

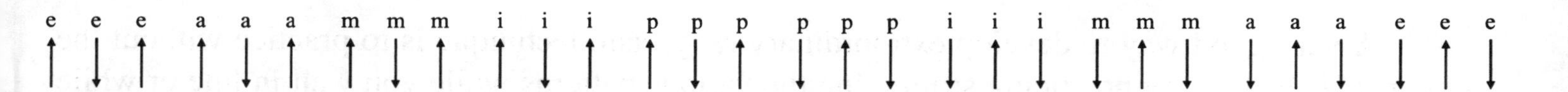

On Practicing the Rasgueado Technique

Now you know more rasgueado patterns that you probably ever thought you would. This is the right moment to examine the best way to practice and internalize them.

Well, the answer is twofold:

1. Slowly!

2. Always using a metronome.

Always practice these techniques very slowly at first, so that your fingers have the time to memorize the motions accurately and there is no hesitation between the different strums. Use a metronome; initially play quarter notes, then 8th notes, 16ths and triplets! This kind of practicing will give you superior control over the rhythmical effect of your rasgueado technique.

What makes a rasgueado sound very impressive and authentic is the evenness of the attack and the "exactly on time" sense. The speed and the power will come as soon as the extensor muscles, which are the muscles responsible for flicking your fingers outwards, get more conditioned and become stronger. This is a process that cannot be rushed!

A very good way to develop extraordinary rasgueado technique is to practice without the guitar. This is done by practicing strumming the various patterns while you wait in line or while walking. I used to practice these patterns while driving, using the safety belt I was wearing as an imaginary guitar. I would put on a tape or listen to the radio, then I would choose a pattern and start strumming it on my safety belt, playing 8th notes, triplets and 16th notes, while trying to stay in perfect time with the music I was listening to. I received a fair share of peculiar looks from fellow drivers, but it really helped improve my rasgueados tremendously.

Also, be careful when first practicing rasgueados. These patterns use the extensor muscles of your right hands, which are usually much less developed that the flexors, the muscles used when plucking notes on the guitar. It is very easy to stress the muscles and overwork them. It is best if the exercises are done conservatively in five-minute sessions. Practice one pattern for five minutes, take a few minutes break, then practice a different one for five minutes and so on.

A Note for Classical guitar players

There are many examples of classical works that require the use of extensive rasgueado technique; here are some of the best known examples:

* Sonatina (3rd movement) - Berkley
* Fantasia Sevillana - Turina
* Ráfaga - Turina
* 3 Short pieces - Rodrigo (Pequena Sevillana)
* Asturias - Albeniz
* Cordoba - Albeniz (as played by John Williams)
* Sonata Meridional - Manuel Ponce
* Verano Porteño - Astor Piazzolla
* Elegy to the Dance - Brower
* Concierto in D - Vivaldi
* Fandango Quintet - Boccherini
* Canarios - Gaspar Sanz
* Rumores de la Caleta - Albeníz
* Concierto d'Aranjuez - Rodrigo
* Concierto de Andaluz - Rodrigo
* Danza del Molinero - Manuel de Falla

Each one of these pieces uses a different rhythmic pattern. Feel free to choose from the options presented in this book and use whichever pattern feels more natural and complements the music better.

Golpe Technique

The Golpe is another technique that has its origins in Flamenco. Its main function is to produce a purely percussive sound from the guitar, by hitting different parts of the right hand on the guitar body. We will examine how to perform two different kinds of golpe on the guitar, in a way that it can be integrated with various rasgueados:

A WORD OF CAUTION: Flamenco guitars come fitted with a *golpeador*; this is a thin layer of clear or white plastic that has been glued on top of the soundboard, just below the high E string. This protects the guitar from being damaged by *golpes*. If your guitar does not have a *golpeador*, be very cautious when using *golpes*, since you can destroy the finish and scratch your instrument very severely.

***Golpes* with the ring finger:**

The most usual *golpe* is performed by the ring finger tapping the soundboard of the guitar, exactly at the corner created by the high E string and the bridge of the guitar. The hand does not move as a whole, only the ring finger moves from the first knuckle. Nail & flesh hit the guitar top at the same time, giving a very characteristic sound. This golpe can be played by itself, or simultaneously with an index downstroke or a thumb downstroke.

Here's an example using the ring finger golpe with an index downstroke. The *golpe* is played every other beat:

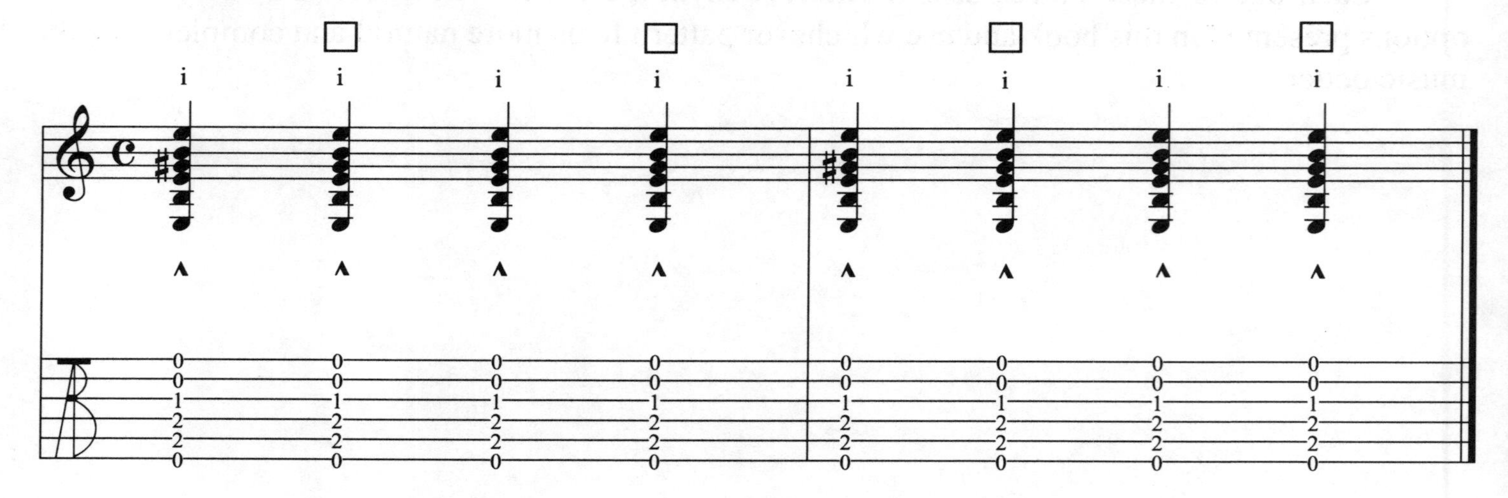

Here's another example using the ring finger *golpe*; this time with a thumb downstroke. The *golpe* is played every other beat:

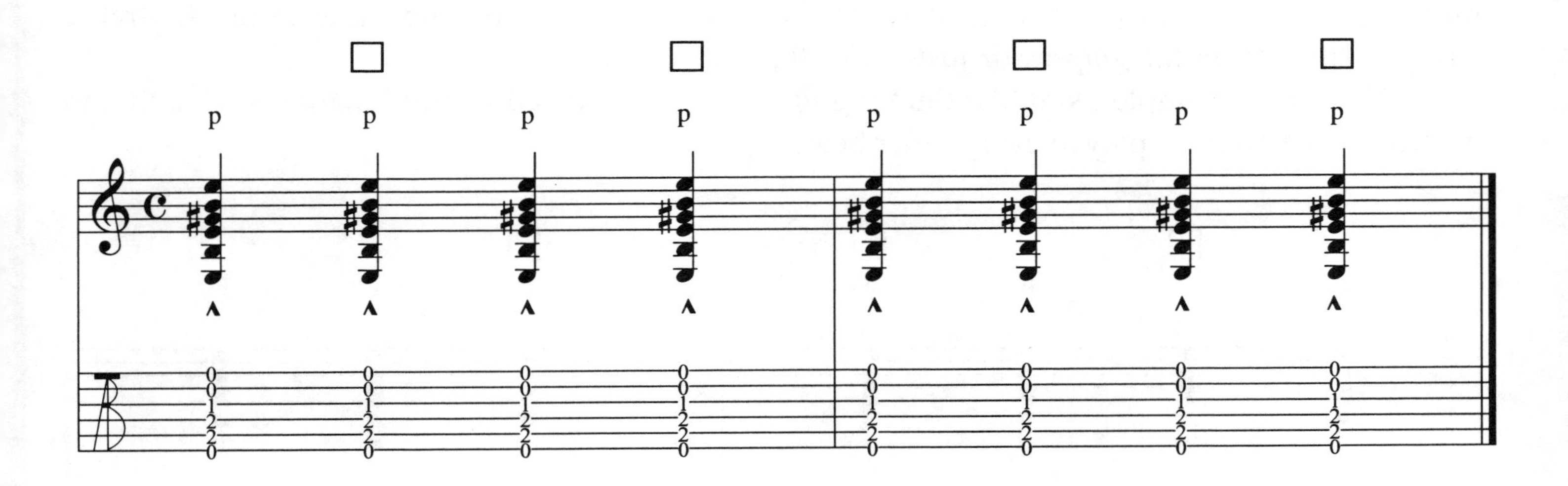

It is also possible to use this *golpe* while playing a single-note line with the thumb. Here's an example based on a traditional Soleares phrase:

Golpes with the Thumb:

A much more unusual, but very effective *golpe* technique is achieved by hitting the *golpeador* with the thumb. While executing any rasgueado pattern that includes an upstroke with the thumb, move your hand slightly lower, so that the thumbnail, on its course upwards to hit the treble strings, will first hit the *golpeador* just below the high E string.

Here's an example using the thumb *golpe*: This is executed in combination with a thumb upstroke. The *golpe* is played every other beat:

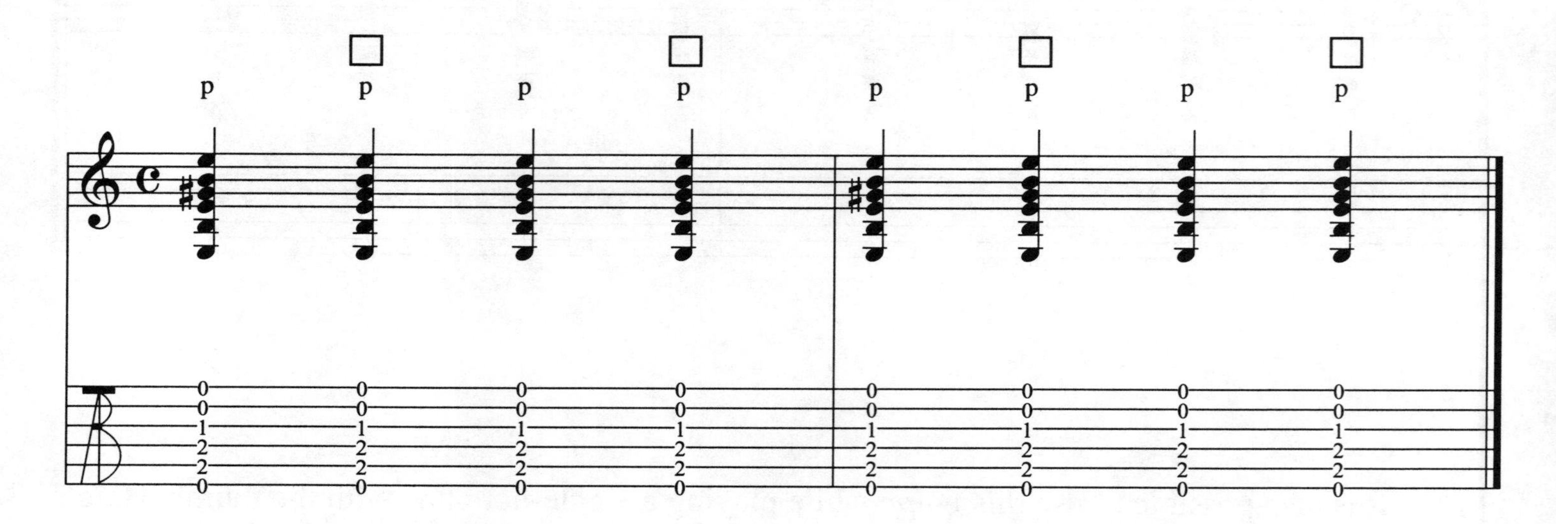

Here's an example, using the *pmp* triplet rasgueado pattern and incorporating a thumb golpe at the beginning of the next beat:

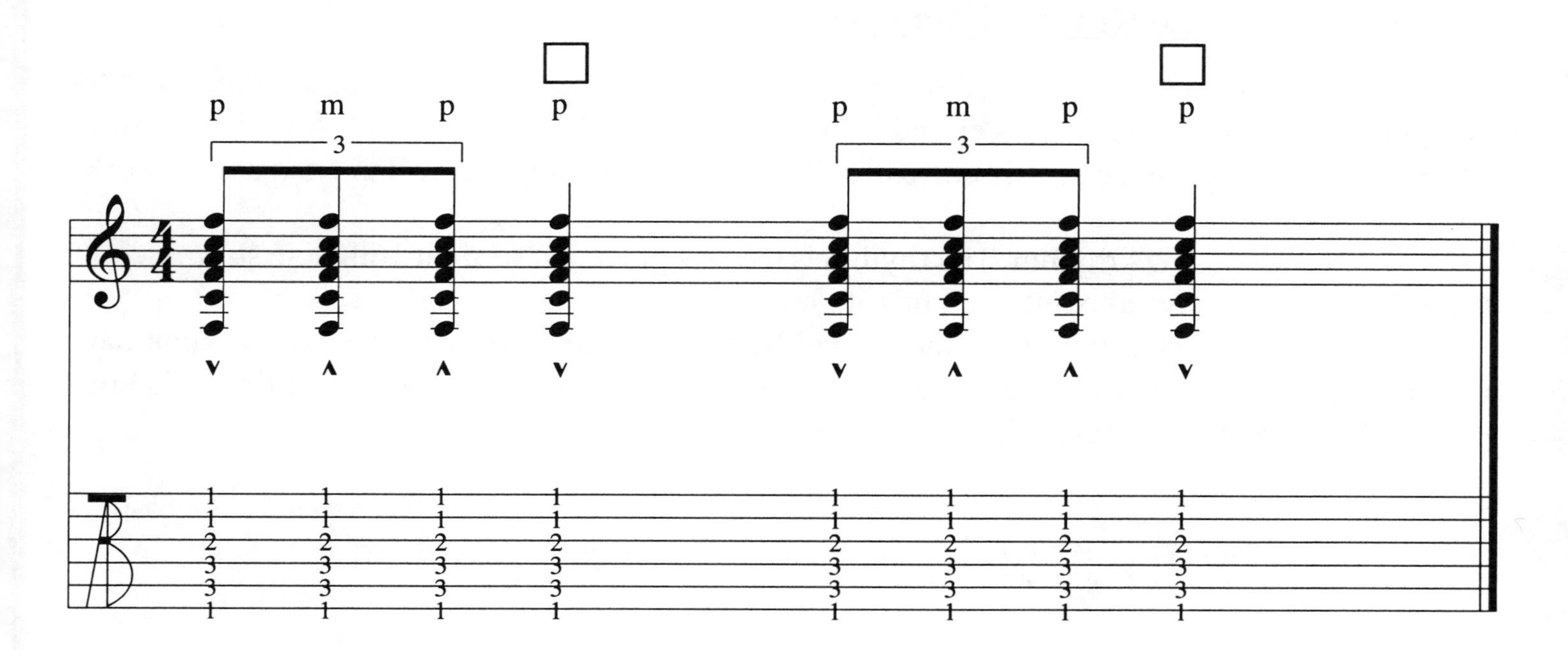

Here's another example, using the *pai* triplet rasgueado pattern and incorporating a thumb golpe at the beginning of the next beat:

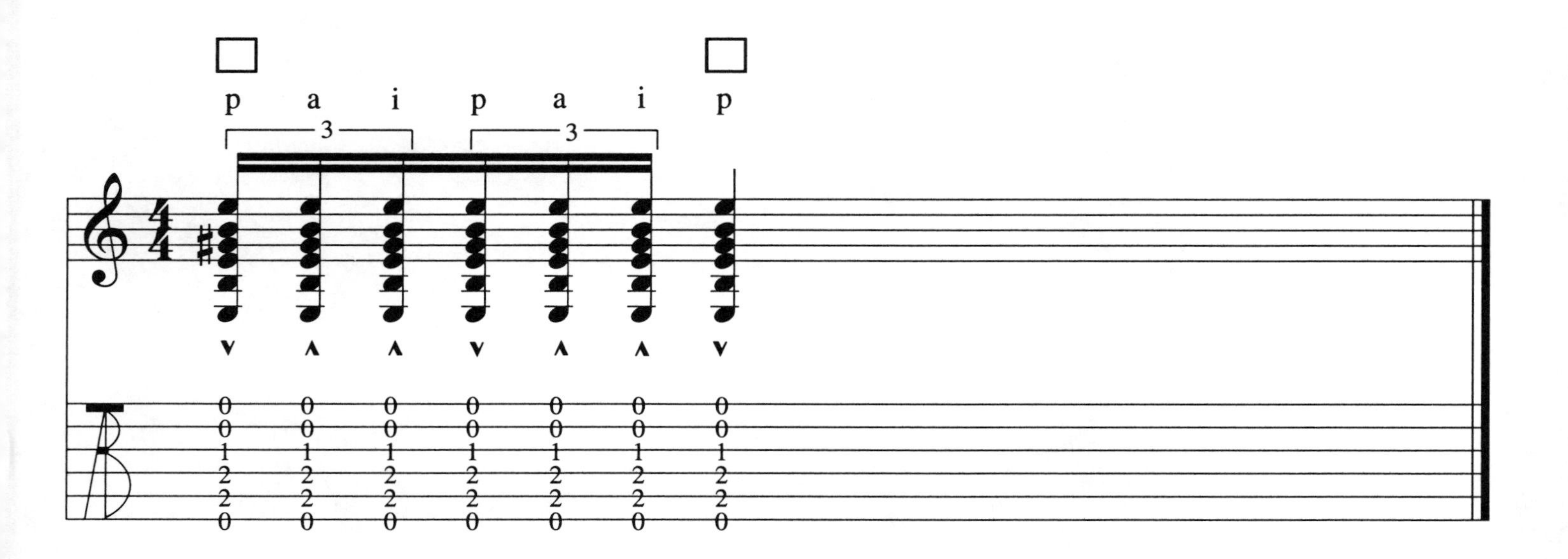

Introduction to the Rumba Flamenca

The rumba is a fairly recent addition to the Flamenco repertoire. The Rumba, along with the Guajira and the Colombiana, are derived from songs brought back from South America by Spanish immigrants and travelers. It is currently the most widely recognized flamenco sound worldwide.

The rumba is a 2/4 rhythm. The rhythm is usually played in straight 16th note strums, so for the 2/4 rhythm we have altogether eight 16th notes.

Usually the first 16th note of the second beat of the rumba is either a slap (the right hand fingers slap all 6 guitar strings just over the soundhole, in a similar way as if swatting a fly) or a golpe. Therefore the rhythm of the rumba is as follows:

From this pattern the 1st and 4th notes of the first beat are more emphasized:

Basic Rumba patterns

Pattern no. 1

Movement description: The hand is in free position. The ring and middle finger joined together play the 1st strum with a downstroke, the thumb plays the 2nd with an upstroke, the ring & middle play the 3rd with a downstroke, and the thumb plays the 4th with an upstroke. Then all the right hand fingers together slap the strings on top of the soundhole (S), in order to stop the sound and create a percussive effect, which last for one 16th note. Immediately, the ring & middle execute an upstroke, then the same fingers do a downstroke and, finally, an upstroke!

It looks very complicated on paper, but it is an easy pattern! Just follow the strumming directions carefully and don't forget that each strum has the duration of one 16th note. This pattern is on of the favorites of the French Gypsy Kings, the remarkably popular rumba masters! Once more, here is the basic rumba pattern:

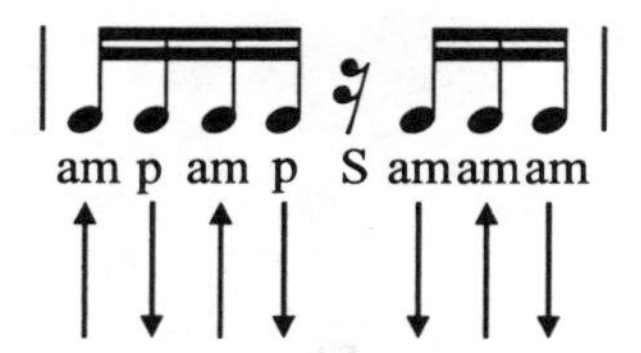

This pattern is the simplest rumba pattern and the one that most beginners learn first. The *am* combination is used to produce a stronger sound than would be possible with a single finger, like the middle finger or the ring finger. The *am* combination is strong enough to create a fairly uniform sound with the thumb, which otherwise would overpower the dynamics of the pattern.

It is very important to realize that it will most probably require quite a few weeks of persistent study before you will be able to produce worthwhile results with this, or any other rumba pattern. Thankfully, once they have been carefully memorized and diligently practiced, these patterns require almost no maintenance drilling.

Pattern no. 2

The first half of this pattern is very similar to the previous one, except the middle finger alone is used instead of the *ma* combination; however, the second half switches to the basic rasgueado position and uses the index finger for the remaining pattern.

Movement description: The hand is in free position. The middle finger plays the 1st strum with a downstroke, the thumb plays the 2nd with an upstroke, the middle plays the 3rd with a downstroke, and the thumb plays the 4th with an upstroke. Then all the right hand fingers together slap the strings on top of the soundhole, in order to stop the sound and create a percussive effect, which last for one 16th note. Immediately, the hand reverts to the basic rasgueado position and the index executes an upstroke, then the same finger does a downstroke and an upstroke!

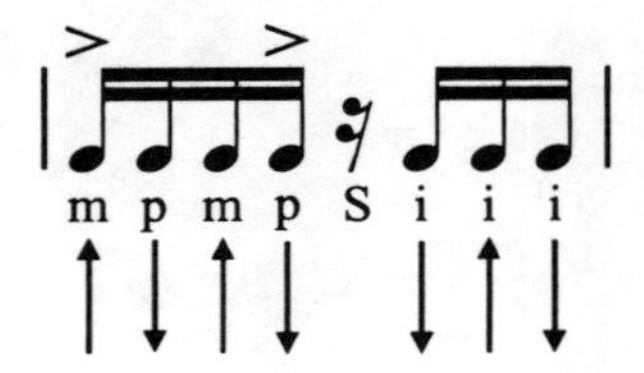

This is a pattern that requires a lighter touch on the guitar strings. This is the reason the middle finger alone is used during the first beat, instead of the stronger middle & ring combination. By using the middle finger, the volume level is kept even with the 2nd half of the pattern, when the index is used exclusively.

Variations on the Rumba patterns

Variation no. 1

Movement description: The hand is in the basic rasgueado position. The index finger plays the 1st strum with a downstroke, while at the same time the ring finger plays a *golpe*. The index plays the 2nd with an upstroke, and the same finger continues and plays the 3rd with a downstroke, the thumb plays the 4th with an upstroke. Then all the right hand fingers together slap the strings on top of the soundhole (S), in order to stop the sound and create a percussive effect, which last for one 16th note. Immediately, the hand reverts to the basic rasgueado position and the index executes an upstroke, then the same finger does a downstroke while at the same time executing a *golpe* with the ring finger and, finally, the index plays an upstroke!

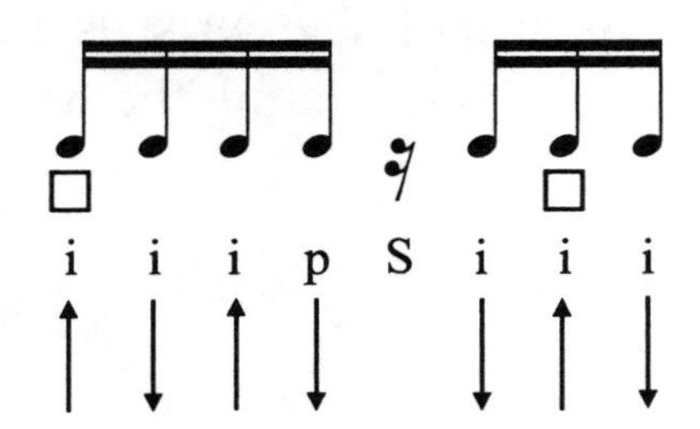

Once more, it looks remarkably complicated when explained on paper, but it is really not a difficult thing to actually perform! Just follow the strumming directions carefully and don't forget that each strum has the duration of one 16th note. The *golpes* happen on the first 16th note and the seventh 16th note.

This is one of my variations on the Rumba rhythm; I find this pattern a little easier to control when I need to switch rapidly from playing rhythm to arpeggios or single note soloing. Another really nice feature is the *golpes*, which add a lot to the effectiveness of the pattern, by providing an extra percussive effect. When performed fast, this pattern is particularly effective.

Variation no. 2

This pattern is a little different, because it starts with a slap (S) on the strings, therefore omitting the first 16th note of the rumba pattern. This is strange, since this is the downbeat of the first beat, usually the strongest and more pronounced beat of all.

Movement description: All the right hand fingers together slap the strings on top of the soundhole, in order to create a percussive effect, which last for one 16th note. Then the ring and middle finger joined together play the 2nd with an upstroke, the same fingers play the 3rd with a downstroke, and the thumb plays the 4th with an upstroke. Then all the right hand fingers together slap the strings on top of the soundhole, in order to stop the sound and create a percussive effect, which last for one 16th note. Immediately, the ring & middle execute an upstroke, then the same fingers do a downstroke and, finally, the thumb executes an upstroke! The wrist is very loose during the execution of this pattern and most of the motion comes from rotating the wrist.

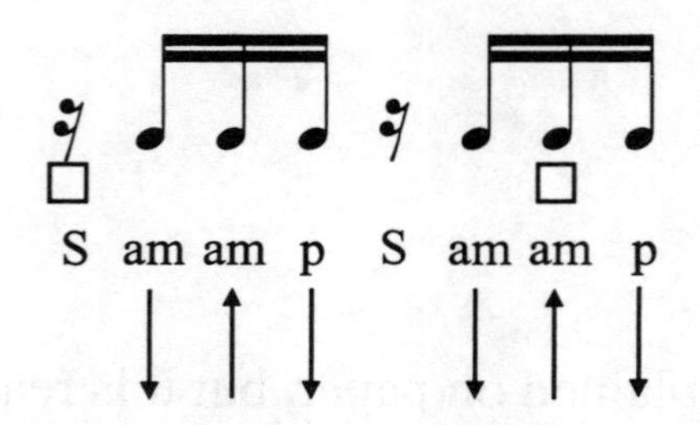

Therefore, this 2-beat pattern is really a 1-beat pattern repeated twice. This is a favorite of the incredible acoustic guitarists Strunz & Farah. It is a very good pattern to use to add some excitement in the rhythm part of the rumba, alternating it with other patterns.

Variation no. 3

This pattern starts with a single bass note, usually the root of the chord being strummed at the time. It also has a rest in the second 16th note of the first beat, in order to let the bass note ring clearly and help establish the tonality.

Movement description: The thumb plays a rest stroke on a bass note, usually the root of the chord being strummed. Then there is a 16th note rest, and then the thumb plays a downstroke, followed by an upstroke. All the right hand fingers together slap the strings on top of the soundhole, in order to create a percussive effect, which last for one 16th note. Immediately, the hand reverts to the basic rasgueado position and the index executes an upstroke, then the same finger does a downstroke and an upstroke!

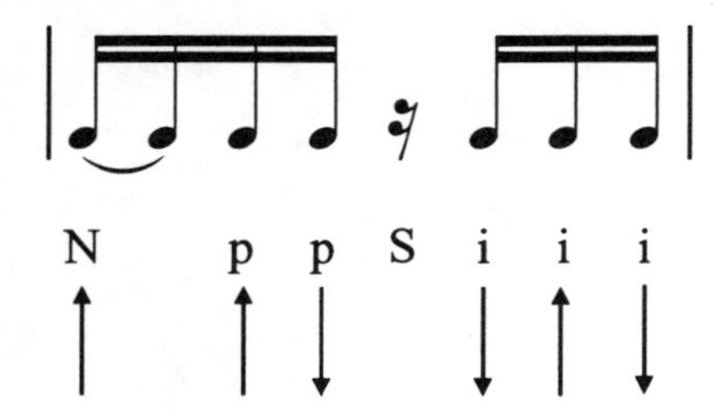

I have found this pattern very effective when playing with another guitar player, who is either playing the melody of the piece, or improvising over the chord progression. The rest of the patterns tend to be very loud and drown the sound of the other guitar player. This pattern however, is rhythmical enough to keep the momentum of the style, but is also dynamically versatile and the single bass note helps define the tonality of the piece.

Variation no. 4

An even more dynamically versatile variation, this next pattern starts also with a single bass note, usually the root of the chord being strummed at the time. This time there is no rest though, but the bass note is allowed to ring clearly for the remainder of the beat!

Movement description: The thumb plays a rest stroke on a bass note, usually the root of the chord being strummed. Then the index executes an upstroke, the same finger does a downstroke and the thumb plays an upstroke that carries over to the first 16th note of the next beat. Then the hand reverts to the basic rasgueado position and the index executes an upstroke, then the same finger does a downstroke and an upstroke.

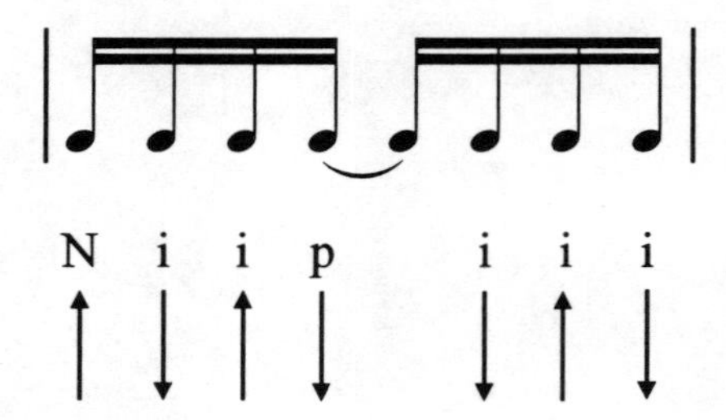

VERY IMPORTANT! During the 1st beat, after the bass note has been played, it is allowed to ring until the thumb plays its upstroke. This is realized by playing with the index finger only the higher strings, so that the bass note will keep on sounding.

This constitutes the vast majority of patterns used for the rumba rhythm. It is important to experiment and develop your own patterns. However, do not neglect practicing the ones outlined above, as they form the basis of this form.

Conclusion

Well, this brings this book into a conclusion. I hope you enjoyed reading this book and learning the rasgueado patterns outlined as much as I enjoyed writing it and researching for it. Rasgueados have always been a personal fascination of mine and I spent a lot of time trying to find the more esoteric and rare ones, dissect them and present them in what I hope to be a clear and concise format.

Keep in mind that even the professional flamenco players do not usually use more that 5-6 different patterns. You don't have to know all of the patterns mentioned in this book, but do try to have a complete repertoire of rhythmic forms you can use in different cases. You should at least know a couple of different patterns to play for each rhythmic variation. For example, learn 2 ways to play triplets, 2 ways to play 16th notes, 2 ways to play quintuplets etc. Start out with the traditional patterns and then move to the rest. But definitely try out all the different patterns and determine which ones fit your hand and your sense of rhythm and timing best. Then practice these slowly and with a metronome until they become second nature and you can execute them effortlessly at will!

Acknowledgements

There are numerous people that I would like to thank, without the help and support of which, I would have never been able to achieve my personal and professional goals. The greatest thanks go to my parents, Efthalia & Konstantinos Anastassakis, for their continuous and multi-faceted support throughout all my years of study.

Very special thanks to my most important teacher and mentor Juan Serrano, the first person to actively encourage me to write this book. To my grandparents Konstantinos & Maria Anassis who instilled to me a deep appreciation of ethnic music from a very young age.

Special thanks to Korina Alivizatou for the beautiful book cover she designed.

Many thanks for their help go to my beloved friends Fotis Bilios, Apostolos Argyropoulos, Natalya Anfilofyeva and Veridiana Sircilli.

I would be unforgivably ungrateful if I forgot to sincerely thank my teachers Stelios Karaminas, Juan Martin and David Oakes.

For the invaluable professional help, many sincere thanks to Angelos Nikolopoulos, Yorgos Foudoulis, Theodosis Temzelides, David Grimes, Gregory Newton, Dr. Ron Purcell, Dr. Steven Gilbert, Michael Murphy and Alain Faucher.

For all the years of inspiration, I am forever indebted to the great flamenco masters Paco de Lucia, Juan Martin, Paco Pena, Serranito, Vincente Amigo, Gerardo Nunez and Sabicas.

About the Author

Ioannis Anastassakis started his musical studies by playing flamenco & jazz guitar at the age of twelve. He studied at the Contemporary Music program of the Philippos Nakas Conservatory in Athens, Greece and continued his studies at the American College of Greece from where he graduated in 1993. Subsequently, he relocated to Hollywood, CA and continued his studies at the distinguished Musicians Institute, where he continued working as a teacher after graduating in 1996.

He continued his studies in Flamenco guitar with Juan Serrano at the California State University, Fresno, where he received an MA in Guitar Performance, graduating Magna cum Laude. Currently, he is working towards a Doctorate degree in education, with emphasis on music at the University of Surrey, UK.

In 1999, he took first prize in the "California Guitar Panorama", an international contest in classical and flamenco guitar.

In 1999, he created in collaboration with the Philippos Nakas Conservatory in Athens the first Flamenco guitar class in Greece.

In 2000, he was the first guitarist ever to present a solo guitar recital at the National Opera House.

He has presented over 250 flamenco guitar recitals in Greece and the United States and has given lectures and seminars at leading American colleges and Universities (*University of Southern California, California State University Northridge, California State University Fresno, California State University Fullerton, Musicians Institute: Fresno City College*).

He has been featured more than a dozen times on American TV.

In Greece he has lectured and performed at the most prominent International Guitar Festivals (*International guitar festival of Ermoupolis, International guitar festival of Volos, International guitar festival of Patras*).

His first solo CD, "**Ioannis - Live at loannina**", was released by MP3.com on August 2000 and immediately entered the company's top ten chart in flamenco guitar music.

Ioannis Anastassakis is sponsored by La Bella Strings.

Presently Ioannis Anastassakis teaches at the American College of Greece and tutors privately around 40 students on a weekly basis. In addition, he is recording his second solo CD for flamenco guitar and preparing a series of books for Mel Bay Publications.

For more information about the artist you can email **info@ioannis.org**

Alternatively, you can visit his Internet site at **www.ioannis.org**

MEL
BAY